Discover more at millsandboon.co.uk.

HIS TWO
ROYAL SECRETS

CAITLIN CREWS

MILLS & BOON

First Published in Great Britain 2019
by Mills & Boon, an imprint of HarperCollins*Publishers*
1 London Bridge Street, London, SE1 9GF

© 2019 Caitlin Crews

ISBN: 978-0-263-08020-9

MIX
Paper from
responsible sources
FSC C007454

This book is produced from independently certified FSC™ paper
to ensure responsible forest management.
For more information visit www.harpercollins.co.uk/green.

Printed and bound in Great Britain
by CPI Group (UK) Ltd, Croydon, CR0 4YY

For Flo, my favorite twin.

CHAPTER ONE

"THE ONLY THING that matters is the line," Crown Prince Ares's dark and intimidating father told him when he was little more than five.

At that age, Ares had no idea what his father meant. He didn't know what line his father was referring to or what bearing it could possibly have on him anyway. At five, Ares had been primarily concerned with how many hours a day he could spend roaring about the palace grounds, out of sight of his nanny, who was forever trying to make him "act like a gentleman."

But he had learned, already and painfully, never to question his father.

The king was always right. If the king was wrong, you were mistaken.

By the time he was ten, Prince Ares knew exactly what line his father was referring to, and was already sick to death of hearing about his own blood.

It was only blood. No one cared if he skinned his knee, but it was clearly very important that he listen to lectures about *the purpose* of that blood. Its dignity. Its import.

When it was still the same blood that welled up

in any scrape Ares might get while doing things he shouldn't around the palace. Things his old nanny liked to tell him were responsible for her gray hair.

"You do not matter," his father would rant during Ares's scheduled appointments with him. "You are merely a link in a noble chain, nothing more!"

The king was forever flinging brandy and various decanters this way and that in his private compartments as he worked his temper into a lather. Ares did not enjoy these appointments, not that anyone had asked him.

And Ares had been schooled repeatedly not to move when his father raged. To sit straight, keep his eyes averted, and refrain from any fidgeting or reacting. At ten, he found this to be a kind of torture.

"He likes a moving target, child," his mother would tell him, her voice cracking as she sat with him, her hands cool against his face and her eyes kind. "You must work on keeping your posture perfect, and never betray your emotions by so much as a flick of an eyelash."

"What would happen if *I* threw something at the wall?"

The queen's smile was always so sad. "Don't do that, Ares. Please."

Ares came to think of it as something of a game. He pretended to be a statue, like the ones that would be made of him someday to grace the King's Gallery that had stood in the Grand Hall of the Northern Palace since—or so the story went—the islands that made up the kingdom of Atilia rose up from the sea. Marble and gold, with a fancy plaque listing his accomplishments.

"Our line has held the crown of Atilia for centuries,"

his father would thunder, while Ares would think, *I am stone*. "And now it rests entirely in your hands. You, a weakling, who I can hardly credit sprung from my own loins."

Stone straight through, Ares would tell himself, his eyes on the windows and the sea outside.

By the time Ares was a teenager, he had perfected the art of sitting deathly still in his father's presence. Perfected it and also complicated it, because he was an adolescent and more certain by the day that he had not one drop of the old king's blood in him—because he hated him too much to be related to him.

"You must never, ever say such things out loud," his mother told him, her voice as exhausted as her gaze was serious. "You must never give anyone in your father's court leave to doubt your parentage, Ares. Promise me."

He had promised, of course. Ares would have promised his mother anything.

Still, sometimes the crown prince was not in a mood to play statues. Sometimes he preferred to stare back at his father with as much insolence as he could muster, wordlessly daring the increasingly old and stooped king to throw something at him. Instead of at the stone walls of the palace, as he usually did.

"You are nothing but a disappointment to me," the king thundered at every appointment—which, thankfully, occurred only a handful of times a year now that Ares was dispatched to boarding schools all over Europe. "Why should I be cursed with such a weak and insolent heir?"

Which, naturally, only encouraged Ares to live down to the worst expectations his father had of him.

Ares accordingly…enjoyed himself. Recklessly, heedlessly, and thoroughly.

Europe was an ample playground, and he made friends in all the desperately pedigreed boarding schools he was eventually kicked out of. Together he and his bored, wealthy friends would traipse about the Continent, from the Alps to the beaches, and back again. From underground clubs in Berlin to parties on superyachts somewhere out there in all that Mediterranean splendor.

"You are a man now," his father told him bitterly when he turned twenty-one. "Chronologically."

By the law of their island kingdom, twenty-one was the age at which the heir to the throne was formally acknowledged as the Crown Prince and Heir Apparent to the Kingdom. Ares's investiture cemented his place in the line of succession, and further, that of his own heirs.

It was more of the same bloodline nonsense. Ares cared even less about it now than he had when he was five. These days, Ares was far more interested in his social life. And what antics he could engage in now he had access to his own vast fortune.

"Never fear, Father," he replied after the ceremony. "I have no plans to appall you any less now I am officially and for all time your heir apparent."

"You've sown enough wild oats to blanket the planet twice over," the king growled at him.

Ares did not bother to contradict him. First, because it would be a lie. He had indeed. And second, because the hypocrisy might choke him. King Damascus was well-known for his own years of sowing, such as it were.

And unlike Ares, his father had been betrothed to his mother since the day of her birth.

It was yet one more reason to hate the man.

"You say that as if it is a bad thing," he said instead, no longer playing games of statues in his father's private rooms.

He was a man grown now, or so everybody told him. He was heir to the kingdom and now would be expected to carry out duties in the name of the crown he would wear one day. He stood by the windows in his father's compartments and looked out over the sloping hills and crystal blue sea.

This would always be Atilia to him. The murmur of the ocean waves. The soft, sweet scent of flowers on the breeze. The Ionian Sea spread out before him.

Not the king and his penchant for smashing things and causing as much distress as he could at the slightest provocation.

"It is time for you to marry," his father intoned.

Ares turned, laughing, and then laughed harder when he saw his father was serious. "You cannot imagine I will be amenable to such a thing. Can you?"

"I have no interest in suffering through the sort of twenties you will inflict upon me. And upon this kingdom."

"And yet suffer you must," Ares replied with a soft menace that was as close as he'd ever come to taking a swing at his father or his king. "I have no intention of marrying."

His father broke a decanter that day that had been in the family since the 1700s. It burst to pieces slightly to the left of Ares, though he hadn't moved a muscle. He'd only stared back at the old man.

But it had broken something in Ares nonetheless.

It wasn't the shards of priceless crystal raining down on his traditional regalia. It wasn't his father's temper, which Ares found little more than tedious at this point.

It was the whole...show. The titles, the land, the bloodline. It all meant more to his father than he ever had. He hadn't been raised by his parents, he'd been monitored by a succession of servants and paraded in front of his father only every now and again. And only when everyone could be certain his behavior was per-fect.

Or tolerable, at any rate.

He couldn't help thinking that really, he would pre-fer not to be a prince at all. And if he had no choice in that, well, there was no need to participate in passing the mantle of blood and nonsense on to the next generation. Ares had no intention of marrying. No interest in it.

But he was adamantly opposed to having children.

He couldn't help but think it was the bloodline it-self that had made his father a monster, coupled with the crown. And he was a monster primarily to his son. He was cold to Ares's mother, but it was Ares who got splintered decanters and rage.

Ares had no intention of passing that rage along to his own children. Ever.

"You should not rile your father so," his mother said years later, after Ares had indulged in yet another con-versation with the king about his marital prospects. He was twenty-six. "We shall have to start importing de-canters from the Southern Palace."

Atilia was an ancient island kingdom in the Ionian Sea. The Northern Island was the most geographically north of the islands that made up the kingdom and was where the business of the country took place. The Northern Palace was accordingly the more stately residence of the royal family. The Southern Palace, on the most southern edge of the most southern island in the kingdom, was about relaxation, not matters of state. Beaches and ease and what breathing room a man could have when the weight of the kingdom sat on his shoulders.

Not that Ares intended to hoist up that weight himself, but still, he preferred the south. It was where he'd been enjoying a few weeks of recuperation after a long goodwill tour before his father had issued his summons. Because clearly too much time had passed between unpleasant conversations about Ares and the bloodline.

"I can't control what riles the man," Ares replied, dryly. "If I could, the last twenty-six years would have been markedly different. And there would be a great many more breakable objects left unattended about the palace, I imagine."

His mother had smiled at him the way she did, soft and sad. Ares always assumed it was because she couldn't save him from his father. She couldn't make the king treat the prince the way he treated her—with icy disinterest. "It is not the worst thing in the world to start turning your thoughts toward the next generation."

"I don't have it in me," Ares told her then. The conviction had been growing in him for years, by then. He studied his mother, and her drawn, dear face. "If you are an advertisement for the institution of marriage, or what one must bear to become queen of these islands, I cannot say that I am greatly inspired to foist this dubious pleasure on anyone."

That was true, but what was more true was that Ares enjoyed his life. He kept a home of sorts in Saracen House, a separate, palatial estate that was part of the palace complex on the Northern Island. But he was never there. He preferred the energy of Berlin. The hustle and rush of London. The mad, thrumming energy of New York City.

Or, really, any place his father was not.

And besides, Ares had yet to meet a woman he wanted for more than a night or two. Much less a lifetime of bloodlines and pomp, tradition and circumstance. He very much doubted the woman who could make him reconsider existed.

Nor was he particularly upset about this lack.

"I see how you are looking at me," his mother chided him. She sat as she always did, upright and elegant, on the chaise in her favorite room of the palace where the sunlight stood in for happiness. Or so it had always seemed to Ares. "And I'm not so old, thank you, that I cannot remember the excitement of youth and the certainty that I could predict the twists and turns of my own life."

"I hope you're not planning to give me any details of the excitement of your youth," Ares said. "Particularly as I was under the impression you spent most of it in a convent."

The queen's smile hinted at secrets, and made Ares glad. He liked to think his mother had more to reflect on in her life than his father and the glacial coldness he knew their marriage contained.

"You must find a wife of similar background," his mother told him quietly. "You are to be the king, Ares. Whatever your marriage is like, whatever bargains you and your spouse make with each other, she must be a queen without stain. So, too, must your issue be without blemish. Do you understand what I'm saying to you?"

He did. But understanding did not equal obedience.

"That I should put off marrying as long as possible," Ares said, and grinned at her. "I am more than happy to oblige."

Ares was halfway through his thirties when his mother died suddenly, lost to a quick-moving cancer she'd thought was a bout of the flu. And Ares was still reeling, still mourning when his father called him back to the Northern Palace some months after the funeral.

"You must know that it was your mother's dearest wish that you married," the king growled, his hand clenched around a crystal glass like it was a weapon. "The bloodline is your most sacred duty, Ares. The time for games is past."

But as it happened, Ares was even less a fan of his bloodline than he had been before. Something he would have thought impossible.

His mother had left him all her papers, which included the journals she had kept since she was a girl. Ares, missing her in the bleak months after her passing, had lost himself in those journals. He wanted to hoard every memory he had of her. He wanted to feel close to her again.

Instead, he learned the truth about his parents. Or about his father, rather, and the royal marriage. Once Ares had been born, they had tried for a spare until the doctors had made it clear that the queen could likely not have any more children. The king hadn't missed a beat. He'd openly flaunted his mistresses.

All those ladies of the court who had cooed at Ares when he was young. All those noblewomen he'd been instructed never to speak with in private. How had he missed their true role?

His father had broken his mother's heart.

Over and over again, every time he took a new woman to his bed.

And Ares had never been overly fond of the king. But this made it worse. This made him hate his father, deeply and irrevocably.

"You betrayed my mother casually and constantly," he said now, his own hands in fists because he did not require a weapon. And wanted only an excuse. "Yet you imagine you can speak to her dearest wishes now she has passed? Do you dare?"

The king rolled his eyes. "I grow weary of coddling you and your refusal to do what is required of you."

"If you're so interested in your bloodline," Ares told him now, "I suggest you expand it on your own, as you seem so predisposed to do. You do not need me to do your dirty work for you. And let me be perfectly clear on this. I will not do it."

His father sneered. "Why am I not surprised? Once a weakling, always a weakling. You would even give away your throne."

But Ares didn't think of it as giving away a throne—

and one he'd never wanted anyway. He was ensuring not only his freedom, but the freedom of any potential children he might have had. He was making certain no child of his would be raised in that cold palace of lies.

And he refused to treat a woman the way his father had treated his mother.

Ever.

His father married again, quickly, to a woman younger than Ares. Ares caused a scandal by refusing to attend the wedding.

The kingdom was in turmoil. The royal advisors were beside themselves.

"The throne has a stain upon it," cried the most senior advisor, Sir Bartholomew. He'd come all the way to New York City to plead his case before Ares, who had refused to grace a room that also contained the king since that last, dark conversation with his father. "The kingdom is reeling. Your father has installed his mistress and dares to call her his queen. And he has claimed that any issue he gets upon her will supersede you to the throne. You cannot allow this, Highness!"

"How can I prevent it?" Ares asked.

He lived halfway across the planet. He spent his time carrying out his royal duties and running the charity he'd started in his mother's name and still enjoying his life as best he could. The tabloids loved him. The more they hated his father, the more they adored what they'd called his flaws as a younger man.

Ares had no intention of submitting himself to his father's court. He had no interest whatsoever in playing the royal game.

"You must return to Atilia," Sir Bartholomew cried,

there in the penthouse suite of the hotel Ares called home
in Manhattan. "You must marry and begin your own
family at once. It is only because your father continues
to refer to you as the Playboy Prince that the people feel
stuck with his terrible choices. If only you would return
and show the people a better way forward—"

"I'm not the king you seek," Ares told him quietly.
Distinctly. And the older man paled. "I will never be
that king. I have no intention of carrying on this twisted,
polluted bloodline beyond my own lifetime. If my father would like to inflict it on more unwary children, I
can do nothing but offer them my condolences as they
come of age."

Ares thought of his mother after his advisors left, as
he often did. What he would not give for another moment or two of her counsel. That sad smile of hers, her
gentle touch.

Her quiet humor that he knew, now, only he had
ever witnessed.

You must marry, he could hear her voice say, as if
she still sat before him, elegant and kind.

And he missed his mother. Ares understood he always would.

But he had no intention of following the same path
his parents had.

He would die first.

His phone was buzzing in his pocket, and he knew
it was more invitations to more of the parties he liked
to attend and act as if he was a normal man, not the
heir to all this pain and hurt and poison. He eyed the
face in his mirror that he hated to admit resembled the
King's, not hers.

Ares straightened his shoulders until his posture was as perfect as she would have liked it, on the off chance she could still see him, somehow. He liked to imagine she could still see him.

And then he strode off to lose himself in the Manhattan night.

CHAPTER TWO

Five months later

"Pregnant?"

Pia Alexandrina San Giacomo Combe gazed back at her older brother, Matteo, with as much equanimity as she could muster.

She'd practiced this look in the mirror. For a good month or two already, and she still wasn't sure she'd gotten it right.

"That's what I said, Matteo," she forced herself to say, in a very calm, composed, matter-of-fact sort of way.

She'd practiced that, too.

"You cannot be serious," her brother blustered, a look of sheer horror on his face.

But Pia was standing before the wide desk in the library of the ancient manor house that had been in her father's side of the family since that early, hardy Combe ancestor had clawed his way out of the textile mills and built it. Or she thought that was how the story went, having always preferred to tune out most of the lectures about the grand history of both sides of her family. Because her parents had so dearly loved to lecture *at* each other, as if their histories were engaged in a twisted battle for supremacy.

And because she was standing there before her brother, wearing a dress that fit her more tightly than she might have liked—in all that unrelenting funereal black that Pia had been draped in for the past six weeks since their mother had died—she could feel it when Matteo's disbelieving stare landed on her belly.

Her belly, which, despite Pia's best attempt to pretend none of this was happening, was protruding. Sticking right out, whether she liked it or not.

There was no way around it.

Her mother, of course, had noticed that Pia was getting "chunky" in the week or so before she'd died. And Pia had learned a long, long time ago exactly what weight she needed to maintain to avoid the acid side of her mother's tongue. Her mother had seen the instant Pia had exceeded that weight, the way she had when Pia had been a rather moonfaced and shy young girl. To the ounce.

Puppy fat is for poor girls with no prospects, the legendary Alexandrina San Giacomo had said to her woebegone twelve-year-old daughter, her magnificent face calm—which made it worse. *You are a San Giacomo. San Giacomos do not have chipmunk cheeks. I suggest you step away from the sweets.*

After that Pia had been so determined to, if not live up to her mother's impossible standard of effortless grace and beauty, at least escape her scathing put-downs. She'd dieted religiously throughout her teens, yet her cheeks had steadfastly refused to slim down, until one morning she'd woken up, aged twenty-two, and they'd gone.

Sadly, she'd taken her fateful trip to New York City shortly thereafter.

And Pia couldn't say why her mother had done what she had done. She couldn't definitively state that it was because she'd discovered her unmarried daughter was pregnant, and on the verge of causing the kind of scandal that was usually her mother's province. Hadn't Alexandrina spent the bulk of Pia's childhood beating it into her—not literally, thankfully, though Alexandrina's tongue was its own mallet—that Pia was to walk the straight and narrow? That Pia was to make certain she remained peerless and without blemish? That Pia needed to be, above all things, Snow White—pure as the driven snow or Alexandrina would know the reason why.

The truth was, Alexandrina hadn't much liked the reason why.

Pia couldn't say that the news that she was not only not at all innocent any longer, but pregnant by a stranger whose name she didn't know, had made her mother decide to overindulge more than usual, as she had. And with such tragic results.

But she couldn't say that wasn't the reason, either.

And now it was six weeks later. Alexandrina had died and left their little family—and her planetful of admirers—in a state of despair. And then her father—brash and larger-than-life Eddie Combe, who Pia had thought was surely immortal—had collapsed with a heart attack three days ago and died that same night. And Pia was certain, now.

This was all her fault.

"You are serious," Matteo said, darkly.

She tried to keep her face calm and expressionless, as her mother always had, particularly when she was at her most awful. "I'm afraid so."

Matteo looked as if he had glass in his mouth. "You are aware, I feel certain, that we are moments away from our father's funeral?"

Pia decided that wasn't a real question. She waited instead of answering it, her hands folded in front of her as if she could stand there all day. She gazed past her brother and out at the Yorkshire countryside arrayed outside the windows, green hills beneath the gunmetal sky. Matteo, his gray eyes more dark and brooding than the stormy sky behind him, glared at her.

But when he spoke again, she had the impression he was trying his best to be kind.

"You look pregnant, Pia."

As if she might have missed that. "I do."

"There will be press at this funeral service. Paparazzi everywhere we turn. There was no avoiding them six weeks ago and it will be even more intense today. You must know what kind of commotion a visible pregnancy will cause."

To his credit, he sounded as if he was *trying* to talk without clenching his jaw like that.

"What do you suggest I do?" Pia asked the question quietly, as if it hadn't kept her up since the night her father had died. If she didn't attend the funeral, would that be worse than if she did?

"How the hell did this happen?" Matteo growled.

Pia had always considered herself close to her

brother. It was only the two of them, after all, caught up some ten years apart in the middle of their parents' famously tempestuous, always dramatic love story. Eddie Combe had been known as much for his tendency to take a swing at his business competitors as for his business itself, Combe Industries, that was the direct result of those tough Combes who'd climbed out of the mills.

Meanwhile, Alexandrina San Giacomo had been the most beautiful woman in the world. That was what they'd called her since she'd been all of eighteen. At her funeral, pop stars had sung elegies, the world had watched the televised version to weep along and post pictures of their black armbands, and rarely a day had passed since without Pia encountering some or other remembrance of Alexandrina that called her *La Bellissima, the angel of our time*.

And that was the more restrained lot.

Their parents' love story had transfixed a generation. Pia had always been transported by it herself, especially as her experience of their love came with the shouting matches, the broken crockery followed by Those Noises behind locked doors, and their utter and complete fixation on each other at all times. No matter who else was in the room.

Matteo, darkly handsome, broodingly intense, and excruciatingly dedicated to his role as the last San Giacomo heir as well as his father's successor in the family business, was precisely the sort of child one might expect to come from such a union.

Pia, by contrast, had been hidden away for most of her life, which she had always assumed was a direct consequence of her chipmunk cheeks. She'd been packed off to a convent, then a finishing school, while everyone in the family had gone to extreme and excessive links to keep her out of the public eye.

They all claimed it was to protect her, but she knew better. She was too awkward. Too chunky. The most beautiful woman in the world could not have an embarrassing, tragic daughter, could she? Alexandrina had been a swan by any measure. Pia was, sadly, still very much the ugly duckling in comparison, and she'd resigned herself to that.

Or she'd tried, very hard, to resign herself to that.

"Did you…ask me how it happened?" She stared at her brother now, feeling the wholly inappropriate urge to let out a laugh. Only her brother's likely reaction to such a thing kept her from it. "Not that you fling it about, or anything, but I was fairly certain you…already knew."

"Thank you for making light of the situation, Pia," Matteo snapped, that glass in his mouth getting the better of him. "I'm glad this is all a joke to you. Our father's funeral starts within the hour. You don't think you could have given me some advance warning about—" his gaze raked over her, and made her cheeks heat with shame "—this?"

"I thought I should do it in person," Pia said. That was true. What was also true was that she really hadn't wanted to do it at all. "And you've been down in London since—" But she didn't want to discuss their mother's death. "And I knew you would be coming up here for the funeral anyway, so I thought, why not wait until I saw you."

And Pia was nearly twenty-three years old. She

might have been protected to the point of smothering her whole life, but she was still a woman grown. So why did she find herself acting like a stammering child when her older brother glared at her?

"This is a disaster," he growled, as if she'd missed that. "This is not a game."

"You're not the one who can't wear most of the clothes in your wardrobe, Matteo," she replied. Airily, because what else could she do? "I don't think you need to tell me how real this is."

He stared at her, shaking his head. And Pia had tried so hard to put a brave face on all this. But the truth was, she was ashamed. She could feel that heat in her cheeks, and everywhere else, too.

And the way Matteo looked at her then, as if he was so disappointed in her it hurt, Pia was very much afraid that she would stay ashamed forever more.

"I'm sorry," she said quietly.

"Who is the father?"

But that only made that sickening shame inside her worse.

"Dad asked me that, too," she said, instead of answering the question.

Because the answer was so…squalid. Humiliating, really. Oh, she'd thought it was so delightful before. She finally had a secret! She was a modern woman at last, like everyone else she knew! She'd stepped smartly into her own future, seized the day—or the night, to be more precise—and had stopped keeping herself like some kind of vestal virgin, forever on the shelf, because for some reason her scandal-ridden family seemed united in their desire to keep her from making the mistakes they had.

Everything was fun and games until the morning sickness hit, she had discovered.

Matteo's glare darkened, which should have been impossible. "Dad knew about this?"

"Both Mum and Dad knew about it," Pia said, her voice small.

Of all the things she couldn't believe, what newly lived inside of her was really the least of it. She didn't understand how the world could continue turning without her parents in it. Her mother had been like the sky above, even in the quiet of her own sitting room. That vast and given to sudden storms. Her father had been like a volcano. Big and imposing, and always *this close* to eruption.

How could they both be gone?

And how could she live with the sure knowledge that she was what had killed them, one way or another?

Her hand crept over her belly, then froze when she saw Matteo's dark gaze follow the movement. A new wave of shame swept over her.

"What..." Matteo shook his head as if he couldn't take all the information in. As if he could make it go away by scowling at it. Or her. "What on earth did they say?"

"About what you'd expect." Pia tried to straighten her shoulders and stand taller, because Alexandrina had always told her it made a girl look a size smaller. "Mum wanted to make sure I knew that it was better to have a boy, as girls will steal your beauty." She opted not to mention the awkward moment that had followed that pronouncement, as Pia and her mother had stared at each other, neither one of them pointing out the obvious. That Pia had clearly done nothing of the kind. Her brother blinked, and she pushed on. "While Dad said, and I quote, 'I should have known you'd turn out to be nothing more than a common tart.'"

She even approximated their father's growl of a voice, with that broad hint of Yorkshire he'd played up, the better to discomfit those who thought they were his betters.

For a moment, Pia and Matteo stared at each other.

Pia felt her stomach turn over, and not with leftover morning sickness. But with disloyalty. Her parents had always had it in them to be awful. Temper tantrums were one of their primary forms of communication. They had always been capable of saying terrible things, usually did, and then went to great lengths to make up for it—usually not by saying anything directly, but with whirlwind trips to far-flung places. Or sudden bouts of affection and sweetness.

They had been disappointed in her. Pia knew that. But if they'd lived, the temper would have given way to something kinder, no matter what they'd said to her in the heat of their initial reactions. She should have said that, too. She should have made it clear she knew they would both have softened.

But it felt too late. For them, certainly.

And for her, the child who had always disappointed them.

Pia could hear the sound of movement in the house outside the library. The staff was getting ready for the gathering that would happen after the service and burial. When all their father's captain-of-industry contemporaries and associates—as Eddie Combe hadn't trafficked in friends—would clutter up the house, pretending they missed him. And all of Europe's heads of state would send their emissaries, because Eddie Combe might have come from the dark mills of Yorkshire, but he had married a San Giacomo. San Giacomos had been Venetian royalty in their time. At least one of their ancestors had been a prince. And that meant that the crème de la crème of Europe was bound to pay their respects today, no matter how little they had cared for Eddie personally.

Pia wanted no part of any of this. And not only because she was terribly afraid that she would cause a commotion simply by appearing in her...state. But because she still couldn't believe her parents were gone. Not when she hadn't had enough time to watch them come round. Not when she'd never know if this time, she'd disappointed them *too much* or if they'd soften the way they usually did. It seemed premature to mourn them.

And deeply unfair that she was expected to do it in public, as if she was part of a show for others to watch and judge.

"Do you not know who was responsible for getting you in this condition?" Matteo asked. Icily. "Or are you simply choosing not to name him?"

And maybe Pia was a little more emotionally fragile than she realized. Because that rubbed her the wrong way.

"I think you'll find that I'm responsible for getting myself into this condition," she replied. "I wasn't attacked, if that's what you mean. Nothing was done to me that I didn't enthusiastically participate in. I'm not a damsel in distress, Matteo."

There was a part of her that might have liked the fact she was pregnant—had it not horrified everyone who knew her. Pia had always wanted a family. Not the one she had, but a real family. The sort that she imagined everyone else had.

Matteo was studying her, and she could almost see the machinery working in his head. "That trip you took to New York. That was it, wasn't it?"

"If you mean the graduation trip I took to celebrate finally completing college, then yes." And oh, how she'd fought for that. It had been Matteo who had finally stepped forward and bluntly told their parents that Pia deserved as much of a chance as anyone to live her own adult life. Her cheeks burned all the brighter. Because she was imagining what he must be thinking of her now. "We had a lovely week in New York. It turns out, I happened to come back home with a little bit extra—"

"I don't understand. You…?"

There was the sound of footsteps beyond the door, and darker clouds began to pull together over the hills in the distance. And Pia stared back at her brother, her cheeks so hot they hurt.

"You don't understand?" she asked him. "Really? I've certainly seen your face and photographs with different women in the tabloids, yet you remain unmarried. How can this be?"

"Pia."

"If you're going to act like we're Victorian, Matteo,

CAITLIN CREWS   31

I should have every right to ask about the state of your virtue. Shouldn't I?"

"I beg your pardon. *I* am not in the habit of having intimate relations with women that I do not know."

"Well. Okay, then." She drew herself up even straighter. "I guess I'm just a whore."

"I doubt that very much," Matteo growled.

But the word stayed in her head, pounding like a drum, because the doors to the library were tossed open then. The staff that Matteo had kept at bay came flooding in, his erstwhile assistant was there to whisper in his ear, and it was time to do their sad duty.

And she knew their father had thought exactly that of her, at least for that moment. He'd looked at her—really looked at her, for a change, because Eddie Combe had usually preferred to keep his attention on himself—only three days before his heart attack. And called her a common tart to her face.

She kept telling herself that wasn't cause and effect. That the heart attack hadn't had anything to do with her condition. And that, if he'd had more time, he would have found her in the next days or weeks and gruffly offer some sort of olive branch.

Yet as she rode down in her brother's car, tucked there in the back with him while he tended to the business of running the family company and his assistant Lauren handled calls for him, she accepted that she couldn't know for sure. How could she?

The last thing Pia knew Eddie had thought about her was that she was a whore. He'd said so. And then in a matter of days, he was dead.

Her mother had called her fat, which wasn't anything new. Then again, that was the worst thing Alexandrina could think to call another woman, and she hadn't yet cycled through to the usual affection before she'd passed.

Either way, Matteo and Pia were orphans now.

And Pia was still terribly afraid it was her fault.

But she snuck her hand over her belly because whether it was or wasn't her fault, that didn't extend to the next generation. She wouldn't allow it.

The funeral service was simple and surprisingly touching. It made Eddie seem far more approachable than he had in life, and Pia wondered if she would understand the man more as time went on. If her memories would mellow him into more of a father figure, lingering on his gruff affection. Or if he would always be that volcanic presence in her mind. The one that had thought his only daughter was a trollop right before he'd died.

The ride back up the hill toward the Combe estate was somber, and Pia was glad, in a fierce sort of way, that it was a moody day. The dark clouds threatened, though the rain held off, and they stood in a bit of a brisk, unpleasant wind as Eddie's casket was lowered into the ground in the family plot.

The vicar, who Eddie had hated in life, though had requested in his will in some attempt to torture the holy man from beyond, murmured a prayer. Pia kept her eyes on the casket that was all that remained of her father—of her childhood—until she could no longer see it.

And somehow kept her tears at bay. Because there were too many cameras. And how many times had Alexandrina lectured her about red eyes and a puffy face?

It hit her again. That Alexandrina was gone. That Eddie was gone. That nothing was ever going to be the same.

Then Matteo's hand was on her back and they moved away from the grave site to form the necessary receiving line for those who might or might not make it back to the small reception at the house. It was times like these that her years in finishing school came in handy. Pia was infinitely capable of shaking hands and making meaningful eye contact with every royal in Europe without noticing them at all.

"May I offer my condolences on the part of the Kingdom of Atilia and His Majesty King Damascus, my father?"

Something about that voice kicked at her.

Pia's hand was already extended. And even as she focused on the man standing before her, his hand enveloped hers.

And she knew that sudden burst of flame. She knew the shiver that worked its way from the nape of her neck down to pool at the base of her spine.

Her eyes jerked up and met his.

As expected, his gaze was green, shot through with gold. And as shocked as hers.

Pia panicked. How could this be happening? The last time she'd seen this man, he had been sprawled out, asleep, in a penthouse suite high above Manhattan. She had gathered her things, feeling powerful and shaken at once by her daring and all the things he'd taught her, and had tiptoed away.

She'd never imagined she would see him again.

"You," he said, almost wonderingly. "New York."

And part of her was warming, in instant response to the way his mouth curved in one corner. As if Pia was a good memory, as he had been for her. At least at first.

Before the morning sickness had sent her to the doctor to discuss the flu she couldn't kick.

But Pia couldn't indulge in memories, good or bad, because she was standing next to her brother. And he was focusing that dark scowl of his on the man still holding Pia's hand.

"New York?" Matteo asked. Demanded, more like. "Did you say you know my sister from New York?"

"Matteo. Stop."

But the man, still smiling slightly, seemed unaware of the danger he was in. "I met your sister in Manhattan some months ago," he said, amiably enough. He smiled at Pia. "Do you go there often?"

"*Miss Combe*, my *younger* sister, has been there once," Matteo growled. "And guess what? She picked up a souvenir."

"I beg your pardon?"

The man frowned. But in that way very important men did, as if inviting everyone around them to apologize for opportuning them.

"My sister is six months pregnant," Matteo bit out.

Pia had the sense that she was in some kind of slow-motion car accident. The sort she'd seen in movies a thousand times. She could almost hear the scraping of the metal, the screech of the tires. Yet everything before her seemed to move in tiny, sticky increments. She watched her brother ball up his fists and step closer to the man. The man—who had told her his name was Eric, though she doubted that was real—did not back up.

And they both turned and stared at Pia as if she was some kind of roadside curiosity.

"If your sister is or isn't pregnant, that is no concern of mine," the man said.

Far less amiably.

Just in case Pia had wondered if it was possible to feel worse about all of this. Look at that! It was. She rubbed at her chest as if that could make her heart stop pounding the way it was. Or at least, ache less.

"Pia," Matteo said, dark and furious. "Is this the man?"

"Have you forgotten where we are?" she managed to ask, though she was barely able to breathe.

"It's a simple question," her brother bit off.

"Once again, the state of your sister's womb has nothing to do with me," the man said.

And he wasn't just *a man*.

If Pia had been going to throw away a lifetime of doing the right thing and making the correct choice over any old man, she would have done it years ago. *This* man was beautiful. Those gorgeous eyes and silky dark hair, a jawline to inspire the unwary into song and poetry, and shoulders to make a girl cry. *This* man had walked into the party where Pia had already been feeling awkward and out of place, and it was as if a light shone upon him. It was as if his bones were like other people's, but sat in him differently. Making him languid. Easy.

His smile had been all of that, plus heat, when he'd aimed it at her, there beneath some modern art installation that looked to Pia's eye like an exclamation point. In bronze.

But best of all, this man hadn't had any idea who she was.

She could always tell. It was the way they said her name. It was a certain gleam in their eyes. But he'd had none of it.

He'd liked her. Just her.

Just Pia.

She'd planned to hold on to that. She'd *wanted* to hold on to that. But it seemed that would be one more thing she didn't get to have.

"Thank you so much for asking about my private life, Matteo," she said to her brother now. In a decent impression of her mother's iciest tone, which came more naturally than she'd expected. "But as a matter of fact, I have only ever had sex with one person."

Then she looked at the man before her, and her memories wouldn't do her any good, so she cast them aside. No matter how beautiful he was. "And I regret to inform you, but that one person was you."

But that didn't have the effect she expected it to have.

Because all the beautiful man before her did was laugh.

At her, if she wasn't mistaken.

"Like hell," he said.

And that was when Matteo punched him.

Right in the face.

CHAPTER THREE

ONE MOMENT ARES was standing straight up, looking one of his past indulgences in the face.

He'd laughed, of course. What could he do but laugh?

Because the truth was, Ares hadn't forgotten her. He hadn't forgotten the way her gray eyes had lit up when she'd looked at him. He hadn't forgotten her smile, shy and delighted in turn. And he certainly hadn't forgotten her taste.

He might even have toyed with the notion of what it would be like to seek her out for another taste, now and again over the past few months—

The next moment he was on the ground, and it took him a moment to understand that the Combe heir had punched him.

Hard.

Not only that, he'd chosen to do so in full view of the paparazzi, all of whom swooped in closer like the locusts they were at the sight. They took picture after picture and held up cameras to record every last detail of the Crown Prince of Atilia's inelegant sprawl across the wet grass in the middle of a funeral.

Ares glared up at the man who had laid him out.

He wanted—badly—to respond in kind, but restrained himself. Because he might not want to be king, but he was still a prince, whether he liked it or not. And princes did not swing on bereaved commoners, no matter the provocation. Moreover, he preferred to control the stories that appeared about him, especially when the press on his father was so dire these days.

He couldn't change the fact this man had hit him. But he could opt not to react in a manner that would only make it all worse.

He climbed back to his feet far more gracefully than he'd gone down. He brushed himself off, his gaze on the man scowling at him in case he started swinging again, then put his hand to his lip. When he drew it away, he noted darkly that there was blood.

Because of course there was blood.

Because everything was about his damned blood. Hadn't his father told him so a thousand times before Ares had turned seven?

Ares noticed movement in his periphery and held up his hand before his security detail handled the situation in a manner that would only make it worse. He glared at the Combe heir, whose name he hadn't bothered to learn as he'd run over his notes on his way here today.

That seemed like a significant oversight, in retrospect.

"You understand that I am the Crown Prince of Atilia, do you not?" he asked coolly instead. "Attacking me is considered an act of war."

"That doesn't frighten me," the other man retorted.

"What should frighten both of you is that this entire conversation is being recorded," Pia hissed at the pair of them.

And that was the thing. He could remember *her* name. Pia.

Such a little name when she had hit him with a good deal more force than her brother had just now.

And the hits kept coming today.

A closer look showed Ares what he should have noticed from the start. That she'd thickened around the middle. And she was a tiny thing—easy enough, if a man had a decent imagination and the necessary strength, to pick up and move around as he liked, and Ares certainly had liked—and her bump was clearly noticeable. Huge, in fact.

It was very clearly…exactly what it was.

But what it could not be was his.

"I have never in my life had unprotected sex," Ares said with as much regal hauteur as he could manage.

The Combe heir looked enraged. Pia only shook her head, her gaze darting around to their audience before returning to her brother.

"If you two want to roll about in the dirt, flinging your toxic masculinity about like bad cologne, I cannot stop you," she said, half under her breath. "But I refuse to become fodder for the tabloids for the first time in my life because of your bad decisions."

And she turned around and marched off, as if it wasn't already too late.

When Ares looked around he could see the speculation on every face within view. Because there had been a punch, and now Pia was leaving, and it didn't take a mathematician to put her belly and him together.

But it was impossible.

"I suggest you follow my sister up to the house," her brother growled at him.

"Or you will do what?" Ares asked, every inch of him the product of at least a millennia of royal breeding. "Punch something again? You do not tell me where I go or do not, Mr. Combe."

"Watch me."

Ares laughed again, more for the benefit of their audience than because he found any of this funny. Or even tolerable.

And then, because he couldn't see another option, he turned and made his way up the long drive that led from the family plot toward the big, hulking house that sat there at the top of the hill. But he took his time, chatting merrily with other guests, as if he was at a party instead of a funeral. As if he didn't have what he suspected was the beginnings of a fat lip.

And as if he hadn't been accused of impregnating a woman by her overprotective older brother, in full view of too many cameras.

He could leave, he knew. No one would keep him here, no matter what Pia's brother imagined. His security detail would whisk him away at a moment's notice.

But Pia's condition was not his doing—could not be his doing—and he felt compelled to make that clear.

He walked inside the manor house, wondering, not for the first time, how it was these northern Europeans could tolerate their stuffy, dark houses. The palaces of Atilia were built to celebrate the islands they graced. The sea was all around, and invited in, so it murmured through every archway. It was there, shimmering, just around every corner.

He asked after Pia in the grand entryway and was shown into the sort of library that made him think of all the headmasters' offices he'd found himself in during his school days. Usually en route to his latest expulsion.

She was standing at the window, staring out at the miserable British countryside, wet and cold. But what he noticed was her back was too straight.

And he didn't know why she would claim that he was the one who'd impregnated her, but it was hard to remember that as he looked at her from behind.

Because he remembered that night.

It had been their second round, or perhaps their third. He had woken to find her standing by the window, wrapped in a sheet from the thoroughly destroyed bed, her fingers against the glass. Manhattan had gleamed and glittered all around. Ares had gone to her as if drawn there by some kind of magnet. He'd brushed aside the weight of her dark, silken hair and put his mouth to the nape of her neck.

He could still remember the heated, broken sound she'd made. Just as he could remember the chill of the glass beneath his palm when he'd braced himself there and taken her from behind—

He shook himself out of that now. Especially when his body responded with as much enthusiasm as he remembered from that night.

"I'm not the father of your baby," he said, his voice grittier than it should have been when he knew he hadn't done this.

"When I realized I was pregnant, I tried to find you,

of course." Pia didn't turn around. She stayed where she was, her back to him and her arms crossed above her swollen belly. He couldn't stop staring at it, as if he'd never seen a pregnant woman before. "It's a decent thing to do, after all. But no matter who I asked, which was its own embarrassment, no one could remember any 'Eric' at that party."

"And because I lied about my name, you think it appropriate to lie yourself? About something far more serious?"

She let out a small sound, like a sigh, but she still didn't turn to face him.

"When I couldn't find anyone by the name of Eric, I thought that was fair enough. Not ideal, but *fine*. I would do it by myself. As women have been doing since the dawn of time. But that's easier to make yourself believe when no one knows. When you haven't yet told your whole family that yes, you had a one-night stand in New York City. And you don't know the name of the man you had that one-night stand with. But guess what? You're pregnant by him anyway."

"It is not my baby."

"But I withstood the shame," she said, her shoulders shifting. Straightening. "I'm figuring out how to withstand it, anyway. I never expected to see you again."

"Clearly not." Ares could hear the darkness in his voice. The fury. "Or you would not dare tell such a lie."

She turned then, and her face was calm. Serene, even. That was like a slap.

Until he noticed the way her gray eyes burned.

"And the funny thing about shame is that I keep thinking there must be a maximum amount any one person can bear," she told him. "I keep thinking I must be full up. But no. I never am."

Something twisted in him at that, but Ares ignored it.

"You cannot wander around telling people that you're having my child," he thundered at her. "This doesn't seem to be penetrating. It's morally questionable at best, no matter who the man is. But if you claim you carry *my* child, what you are announcing is that you are, in fact, carrying the heir to the Atilian throne. Do you realize what that means?"

Pia looked pale. "Why would I realize that—or anything about you? I didn't know who you were until fifteen minutes ago. Much less that you were a *prince. Are* a prince. A *prince*, for God's sake."

A man who had renounced his claim to a throne should not have found the way she said that so…confronting.

Ares pushed on. "Now you know. You need to retract your claim. Immediately."

"Are you denying that we slept together?" she asked, her voice shaky.

"We did very little sleeping, as I recall. But I don't see what that has to do with anything."

"I've only ever slept with one man," she threw out there. "You."

Or so it seemed to Ares as it sat there, bristling in the center of the library floor.

The implications of that statement roared in him.

But Pia was still talking. "If you are not the father, we have a far larger problem on our hands." She even smiled, which made the roaring in him worse. "Shall I contact the Vatican to notify them of the second immaculate conception? Or will you?"

Ares stared back at her as that scathing question hung in the air between them, too, joining in with all the rest of the noise. The roar of it. And it wasn't until that moment that he realized that for all he liked to think of himself as an independent creature, in no way beholden to crown or kingdom unless he wanted to be, he really was a prince straight through.

Because he was wholly unaccustomed to being addressed in such a manner.

It had never occurred to him before this moment how very few people in his life dared address him with anything but the utmost respect. Yet today he had been punched in the face. And was now being spoken to in a manner he could only call flippant.

Pia swallowed as he stared at her, and then wrung her hands in a manner that suggested she was not, perhaps, as sanguine as she appeared.

Ares didn't much like what it said about him that he found that…almost comforting.

"Happily," she said in a low voice, "it doesn't matter whether you believe me or not. There is a selection of tests to choose from to determine paternity, both before and after birth."

"It is not a question of whether or not I believe you."

"I'm not sure I blame you," she said, as if he hadn't spoken. Another new experience for Ares. Especially as she sounded as if she was attempting to be *generous*. "I can see how such a thing would be difficult to believe if I was…like you."

Ares's brow rose and he suspected he looked like all those pictures of his lofty, patrician, infinitely regal ancestors. "Like me?"

"I doubt you remember the particulars of our night. Or me. And why would you? You must have such adventures all the time."

He might have been caught on the back foot since he'd arrived in Yorkshire this afternoon, but he wasn't foolish enough to answer that question.

"Here is what I don't understand," he said instead, as a sort of low, heated pounding started up in his chest, then arrowed out into his limbs. His sex. "You claim you were innocent before that night. Why? You're not a child."

"Do children prize chastity? Or is it their natural state?"

"I could not say if they prize it or do not," he growled. "I know I never did. I shrugged it off at the first opportunity. I was under the impression that was the entire purpose of the boarding schools I attended." He prowled toward her, keeping his eyes fast on hers. "Were you locked away in a convent, Pia?"

Something like humor flashed across her face. "Yes."

That startled him. He came to a stop before her. "An actual convent? Complete with nuns?"

"Of course with nuns. It couldn't very well be a convent without nuns, could it?"

"What on earth were you doing in a convent?"

She looked wry. "Protecting and defending my honor and holding fast to my chastity, of course. What else?"

"And what? The moment you walked through the convent doors into the big, bad world, you decided the time was ripe to rid yourself of that pesky hymen? With the first man you laid eyes upon?"

He ignored the other thing in him, dark and male,

that didn't like that idea. Because Ares was not accustomed to being *any man*, indistinguishable from the rest. Notable only because he was male.

"First I went to finishing school," Pia said, and for all that her eyes were too big, and her face was pale, Ares noticed that she didn't back down. "There I learned excruciatingly important things. A bit of political science and economics to pepper my banquet conversation, and how best to talk about books to make myself seem important and intellectual, yet approachable. I learned how to dance graciously, as befits a hostess and guest at any gathering. I learned the various degrees of curtsies, and when to employ them. I was meant to be a kind of weapon, you understand."

"I do not understand." But he was too close to her now. He couldn't seem to pull his eyes away from her. There was not one part of him that wanted to, for that matter, and he remembered that magnetic pull, that night. How could it still affect him? "But I'm feeling the effects of your bombshell, nonetheless."

"I graduated six months ago," Pia said quietly, her chin lifting as she held his gaze. "My friends and I decided to take a trip to New York to celebrate. One of my friends knew the person who was throwing that particular party. And there you were. See? There's nothing nefarious."

"Save the fact that I have had what I could only term an epic amount of sex in my lifetime, *cara*," he said, almost drawling the words. "But no one has ever turned up claiming I left them pregnant."

"I didn't actually 'turn up.' You did. Here. At my father's funeral." Her gray eyes glittered. "But by all means, let's brush that aside and continue to talk about your feelings."

"It is not a question of feelings," he said, through his teeth. "It is a question of what is possible and what is not."

She lifted a shoulder, then dropped it. "There is only one possible way I could have gotten pregnant. Because there was only the one night. And only the one man."

"But I do not—"

"Please." Those big, gray eyes implored him, though the hand she held up was rather more of a demand. "There's no point arguing about this. Why don't you give me your details and I'll arrange a test. No point discussing it further until then, is there?"

"Pia. You cannot imagine that I will simply wander off into the ether, can you?" He didn't know what possessed him. One moment he merely stood there a foot or so away from her. And in the next, his hands were on her delicate shoulders, holding her there as if she'd tried to walk away. When he should have wanted that. "Or is that what you want me to do?"

A strange expression moved over her face, darkening her eyes. That wry twist to her lips was back, and deeper this time.

"That's a question you need to ask yourself, I think," she said softly. "In the absence of a test, who's to say who's the father is? I certainly won't say a thing, no matter who asks."

That dropped through Ares like a stone. A heavy weight, sharp and cold and jagged, sinking deep inside him.

He could turn around and leave, right now. His lip would heal. The tabloids would speculate, but then, they always did. If he didn't feed them, surely the stories would die away.

And he could carry on as he'd always intended. As he'd planned.

But despite himself, he thought of his mother.

Of how disappointed she would be in him if she were here.

Nothing had been more important to the queen than her family. Him. All she had ever wanted for him was a wife. A child.

He could shrug off his father's obsession with bloodlines without a second thought, and had. He'd shrugged off his father as easily.

But never his mother.

Never.

He realized his hands were still wrapped around Pia's shoulders. Her head was tipped back, and that belly of hers was between them.

And he wanted nothing to do with this. He wanted to turn back time, refuse to come to this funeral, or go back further and make sure he was nowhere near that party in Manhattan that night.

Even if that would have meant missing out on that taste of her that haunted him still, loathe as he was to admit it.

"There are two things you must know about me," he told her gruffly, as if he was making vows. "First, I have no intention of marrying. My father, the king, would love nothing more than to knock me out of the line of succession entirely. And I have done my best to help him with that, as it is preferable to playing his little games. And second, but just as important, I had no intention of ever having children."

"Is this the royal version of congratulations?" she asked, but her voice quivered. He could feel it inside him, like shame. "It needs a little work."

"I want no part of this," he told her, dark and sure. "But I will do my duty. One way or another."

Ares wasn't sure what he meant by that. All he could seem to concentrate on was that he'd moved too close to her without meaning to. His mouth hovered worryingly close to hers. He could so easily tilt himself forward and help himself to those lips of hers, impossibly sweet and soft and *right there*—

But Pia twisted her shoulders and stepped back, out of his grip. He could have held her fast, and knew full well he shouldn't have felt a sense of heroism that he hadn't. And then he felt something far worse crawl through him as her hands went to cover her belly.

As if she was protecting her child from him.

His child, if what she said was true.

"I haven't asked you for anything," she said, very distinctly. Quiet, but sure. "Including your reluctant, begrudging sense of duty, thank you very much."

The door behind them opened, and Ares turned, astonished that anyone would dare interrupt him.

It was a day for astonishment, it seemed.

"Your Highness," the head of his security detail said, bowing his head apologetically. "I'm afraid there is a situation with the paparazzi. We must go."

CHAPTER FOUR

PIA FELT AS IF she had whiplash. Everything had been in hideous slow motion at her father's graveside, but now, it was as if events were tumbling of their own accord. A glance out the window showed the scrum of reporters, all shouting and shoving. Her gut felt much the same.

She felt as if she was a train on a broken track, careening out of control.

Though she knew better. There was no train. Events weren't carrying on of their own volition. And while she might feel out of control, that didn't make it so.

It was him.

Prince Ares.

His name was not Eric. It had never been Eric. And now that she knew who he was, she couldn't quite imagine how she'd believed he was just…some guy. That he was royal appeared stamped deep into him, today. How had she missed it in New York? It was the way he stood. It was the way he lifted that imperious brow of his. It was the way he assumed command, instantly.

He drew her back from the window. He barked out an order to his guard, then returned his considerable attention to her, green and gold and grave.

How had she convinced herself there was anything *regular* about this man at all?

"We cannot get to the bottom of this here," he told her in a tone that matched the expression on his face. And made everything in her careen about all the more. "You will have to come with me."

"Come with you?" she repeated, dazed. "What do you mean? Where?"

But Ares did not wait for her acquiescence. Perhaps he assumed it wasn't necessary. Perhaps, where he came from, agreement with his every whim and desire was the law of the land. He certainly acted as if it was. He strode off, his long legs eating up the floor of the library in only a few strides. And then he stopped at the door, turning back to her with that astonished, arrogant look of his.

"Pia. That is your name, is it not?"

In case she'd forgotten that every single part of this situation shamed her and humiliated her.

"It is, yes," she said, threading her fingers together and making herself smile the way she'd been taught. Serene and smooth. "And in all the confusion and violence, I believe I missed your formal introduction. You are...?"

She watched that hit him, like a slap. He blinked as if it had never occurred to him that any person alive might not know precisely who he was—suggesting that he'd thought she was only pretending not to know him in New York.

Pia should have been more sympathetic. After all, she knew what it was like to be known, often when she would have preferred to be anonymous. She knew what it was like to have an inescapable family identity that followed her around and often preceded her. And possibly, if she had been a better sort of person, she wouldn't have taken such enjoyment in watching Ares's struggle.

Alas.

"I am His Royal Highness, Crown Prince Ares of Atilia. Duke of this, Earl of that. But no need to address me by my full title. Ares will do."

He certainly didn't appear the least bit ashamed that he could have spent a night like that with someone and not know their name. Pia resolved she should feel no shame herself.

And while she couldn't quite get there, she could certainly fake it. She lifted her chin and tried to exude a sunniness she didn't quite feel.

"It's lovely to meet you, at last," she said. "But you should know that I have no intention of going off somewhere with you. I did just meet you, after all."

And she remembered every scandalous searingly hot detail of the night she'd spent with him. She had seen all kinds of expressions cross his face. She had seen him laugh, go tense and hot, shatter.

But she had never seen him look *dangerous* until now.

"You do not understand, so allow me to enlighten you." His voice was almost as striking as that expression on his face. Dark. Powerful. Nothing lazy or offhand about him, and his green eyes blazed. "You have made a claim to the throne of the kingdom of Atilia. If what you say is true, you are pregnant with my child."

"What does it matter?" she asked, with a brazen sort of calmness she did not feel. "You said you have no intention of marrying. And so what if you have illegitimate children? Don't all kings litter them about, here and there, down through the history books?"

His perfect, sculpted lips thinned and if possible, his gaze grew hotter. And more dangerous. "Atilia is an ancient kingdom, bound by ancient rules. I cannot imagine you truly want a lesson in our laws and customs regarding succession."

"I'm certain I didn't ask for a lesson in anything."

He ignored that. Or didn't care, more likely. "Legitimate issue takes precedence over illegitimate issue. But only if they are male."

"What a shock."

"I am next in line to the throne. Any legitimate child of mine would ascend that throne after me. In the absence of children, a line of succession would move on. Either to any children my father's second wife produces, or to my cousin. If any children I have are illegitimate, they would precede my father's second round of children only if my father had girls."

"That is a fascinating history lesson. Thank you." She smiled at him still, though it felt more…fixed, somehow. "An alternative would be for you to go away. And never tell anyone. I will do the same. And we will never again talk about *issue*."

Or anything else, she thought stoutly. And waited to feel relief rush in.

But instead, she felt something far more bittersweet flood her, though she couldn't quite name it.

"I'm afraid it is much too late for that, Pia," Ares said, with that quiet power of his that shook through her no matter how solid she told herself she was. "Because speculation already exists. Reporters clamor outside even now. What they cannot learn for certain, they will make up to suit themselves."

"You must know the folly of living your life by what the tabloids say," she chided him. Gently.

"I never have."

"Wonderful." She smiled. "Then no need to start now."

"You said yourself that you have never appeared in the tabloids before. There is no reason to throw yourself in the midst of a nasty little scrum of them, like a bone to pick."

If Pia didn't know better, she might have been tempted to think he was trying to protect her.

"More than that, there were reporters who heard you make your claim," Ares said. He shook his head. "Do you know nothing of the history of this planet? Wars have been fought for much less than a claim to a throne."

"You talk about war a lot," she said, and felt herself flush when his gaze turned considering. "In case you were unaware."

"I am a prince. One of my main roles in this life is preventing wars from ever taking place. One way to do that is to conduct my private affairs *in private*." He inclined his head, though Pia was aware it was a command and not a sign of obedience or surrender. "My car awaits."

"And if I refuse to get into it with you?"

"I have a security detail who will put you in the vehicle, no matter your protests. But you know this." Again, that dark, considering look that seemed to peel her open. "Is that what you want? Plausible deniability?"

For a moment, Pia didn't know what she wanted. She

felt the way she had when her doctor had come into the exam room and told her the news. Pia had been fairly certain she was dying of something. All those strange cramps. The fact that she kept getting sick. She was certain something was eating her away from the inside out.

It had never occurred to her that she could be pregnant. The word itself hadn't made sense.

She'd made the doctor repeat herself three times.

Looking at Ares, here in the library of Combe Manor where she had spent so much of her childhood, was much the same.

That train kept jumping the tracks and hurtling away into the messy night, no matter how still she stood or how gracefully she tried to hold herself together.

But she could hear her brother's clipped tone from the other side of the door, issuing his own orders. She'd seen that scrum of ravenous reporters out in front of the house, clamoring for a comment and ready to pounce.

"Let me tell you what sort of life you will lead," her mother had said in the days following her graduation from finishing school, right here in this very same manor house, stuffed full of pictures of all the battle-hardened Combes who had charged out of their circumstances and had *made something of themselves*, no matter what.

Pia knew she was meant to feel deeply proud of them all. When instead, all that desperate clawing for purchase made her feel...tired. And unequal to the task.

"Am I supposed to know what to do with my life?" Pia had asked. "I can't seem to make up my mind."

"It's not for you to decide, dear girl," said her mother, who only called Pia *dear* when she was in one of her less affectionate moods. Pia had sat straighter, waiting for the inevitable other shoe to fall. "Your father has gone to a tremendous amount of trouble to make you into the perfect heiress. Biddable and sweet enough. Reasonably accomplished in the classic sense of the term. And very, very wealthy, of course."

It had seemed wiser not to say anything. Pia had sat there at the breakfast table off the kitchen where her mother drank her hot water and lemon, murmured about how refreshed she felt with each sip, and raised her brows at Pia's slice of toast with a bit of creamery butter.

Which was to say, it was a normal breakfast at Combe Manor. Pia could have drunk the hot lemon water herself, but she'd long ago learned that it was better to disappoint her mother as early in the day as possible, so there could be no grand expectations over the course of the day she would then fail to meet.

Alexandrina had let her gaze sweep over her daughter as if she was sizing her up for market. "You will work in some or other worthy charity that we will vet, of course. You will dedicate yourself to your good works for a year, perhaps two. Then I imagine your father will suggest a suitor. He might even allow you to pick one. From a preselected group, of course."

"You make it sound as if he plans to marry me off."

Pia had spent much of her life despairing over the fact that while she had the same dark hair and gray eyes as her mother, Alexandrina's all…came together. She was simply beautiful, always, no matter what. It was a fact, not a to-do list. Pia had the raw material, but she was put together wrong. No matter how hard she tried to glide about, exuding effortless beauty.

"Dear girl, your brother will run the business," Alexandrina had replied, as if Pia had said something amusing. "He is already in line to do so. You are here to be decorative, or if not precisely decorative—" the look she'd slid at her daughter had been a knife, true, but Pia had been so used to the cut of it she hadn't reacted at all "—you can be *useful*. How will you accomplish this, do you think?"

Pia hadn't had an answer for her. Her accomplishments, such as they were, had always been a serene collection of tidy, unobjectionable nouns. She'd no idea how one launched off into a verb.

"What did you do?" she asked her mother instead.

She already knew the story, of course. Her father liked to belt it out at cocktail parties. Alexandrina had been set to marry some stuffy old title of her father's choosing, but then she'd met Eddie. First they'd made headlines. Then they'd made history, uniting the brash, upstart Combe fortune with the traditional gentility of the San Giacomos.

Pia rather doubted that an epic love story was in the cards for her. Epic love was the sort of thing that *just happened* to women like her mother, and led to decades of *true love*. Which in the San Giacomo/Combe family had always meant operatic battles, intense reunions, and a revolving door of scandals and sins. Pia had always thought that, really, she'd be quite happy to find herself *reasonably content*.

"You and I are not the same," Alexandrina had said softly that day, something making her gray eyes glitter. "And I can see that you think I'm being cruel to you. I am not."

"Of course not," Pia had agreed, staring at her plate and wishing she could truly rebel and order a stack of toast instead of her one, lonely slice. But she only dared antagonize her mother—who despaired over Pia's sturdy figure, inherited from the Combe side of the family and suitable for factory work, not fashion—so far. "I don't think that at all."

"We have wrapped you up in cotton wool as a gift, Pia," Alexandrina had intoned. "Always remember that."

Pia remembered it, all right. She'd decided she wanted no part of any cotton wool, so she'd charged right out and shed it in New York. Enough with *nouns*, she'd thought. She wanted to be about *verbs*, for a change.

And look what that had got her.

"You look as if you're mulling over a very important decision," Ares said, still watching her from the door. "But you must realize that you have no choice here."

"It's out of the frying pan, into the fire."

Pia hadn't meant to say that out loud. But there it was, dancing between them.

Ares didn't reply with words. He only inclined his head in that way of his, that she already knew was him at his most *royal*. Too royal to live, really.

And Pia thought of her father, blustering and brash Eddie Combe, who had called her names and then died. She would never see him smile at her again. She would never stand there while he blustered and bullied, then softened. He would never pat her on the head the way he had when she was small and tell her things like, *Buck up, girl. Combes don't cry.*

But another thing her father had said, so famously

that the vicar had quoted him in the service today, was that if the worst was coming, you might as well walk into it like a man rather than waiting for it to come at you as it pleased.

Control the conversation, Eddie liked to say. And had said, often.

And then did.

Pia told herself that was why she moved then, walking across library floor as if she was doing the bidding of her unexpected prince. That was why she followed after him, ignoring her brother and their guests as his staff led them through the manor house, down and around to the servants' entrance, far away from the mess of reporters out front. That was why she got into the car that waited for them there, meekly and obediently, and sat next to Prince Ares as he drove her away.

It wasn't capitulation, she assured herself. She was *controlling the conversation*.

And it certainly had nothing at all to do with the way looking at those green eyes of his made her heart thump wildly in her chest.

Or that melting feeling everywhere else.

CHAPTER FIVE

PIA REGRETTED HER impulsiveness the moment the car started moving.

She regretted it as they left Combe Manor behind, taking the little-used back road off the hill and leaving the paparazzi—and her brother, and her entire life— behind them.

Pia told herself she was only getting a few tests. That she wasn't leaving anything, not for long. That this would all be perfectly fine once she and Ares were on the same page and plans were made for the future.

But she couldn't shake the sense of foreboding that squatted on her, there on the smooth leather seats of the royal town car.

The car swept them off to a private airfield, and Pia dutifully trooped up the stairs into the jet that waited there, assuming that the prince would take them off to London. Where there were doctors aplenty who could administer the necessary tests, and give him the answers she already had, but he needed to see on official letterhead of some sort or another.

She told herself that she didn't mind that he needed proof. After all, wasn't that at the crux of all this? He didn't know her. She didn't know him. That would per-haps suggest that they shouldn't have slept together, but they had, and it was only to be expected that he would require proof. Even if he really had been just some guy named Eric.

But the sound of the jet engines lulled her to sleep, and when Pia woke again because the air pressure was making her ears pop, she felt as if she'd been sleeping for a very long time.

"Where are we?" she asked sleepily, because a glance out the window into the dark didn't show the mess of lights she would expect above a city like London.

Ares sat across from her on one of the royal jet's low, gold-embossed leather couches.

"We will be landing shortly," he said, without look-ing up from his tablet.

Pia always forgot that her body had changed, and kept changing. She went to sit upright and struggled a bit, certain that she looked as ungainly and inelegant as she felt.

"Yes, but where?" she asked, hoping her business-like tone would divert attention away from what her mother would have called her *persistent ungainliness*. "That can't be London, can it?"

Down below the plane, there were great expanses of darkness, and a few lights. They were headed toward the light, but it was far too contained to be a city.

"It is not London," Ares said, something in his voice making her turn her head around to look at him directly. "It is the kingdom of Atilia. My home, after a fashion. I'm taking you to the Southern Palace."

"But… Why on earth would you take me…?"

"Where did you imagine I would take you?"

He considered her, and she became *aware*—in a hot rush that made her cheeks flare into red—that they were, for all intents and purposes, alone in this compartment of his plane. His security detail had stayed in the main bit, while Ares had escorted her here and closed the door. She had no idea how she had possibly slept so deeply when Ares was right here, taking up all the oxygen.

And that was all before she started thinking about the ways this man could *take* her.

Not to mention the ways he already had.

"I assumed, reasonably enough, that we would pop down to London."

"London is far too exposed. Here in the islands I can control who sees you and me together, what conclusions they might draw, and so on. And I can have my own doctors administer any tests."

"I didn't bring anything," Pia protested. And when that aristocratic brow of his rose, as if she wasn't making any sense, she felt her face get hotter. She cleared her throat. "Like a passport."

"I am the Crown Prince," Ares said dryly. "I do not suffer bureaucracy."

"Because you are the bureaucracy?"

She regretted that. Especially when all he did was fix that overtly calm green gaze on her, making her want to squirm about in her seat. She refrained. Barely.

"And after I take all the tests you need me to take?" She blinked a few times, trying to clear her head. And the sleep from her eyes. "My life is in England."

"If by some chance you are truly carrying my child

and the unexpected heir to the kingdom of Atilia," he said, with something far too complicated to be simple temper in his voice, "then you can be certain that life as you know it has changed irrevocably."

"Well, of course it has," Pia said. Crossly, she could admit. "But it has nothing to do with you. Impending motherhood generally changes a girl, I think you'll find. It's fairly universal."

The jet was dropping closer to those lights below, and Pia felt something like panic clawing at her. Maybe that was why she didn't wait for him to answer her.

"You can't spirit me away to an island and keep me there, Ares," she said instead. But if she was looking for some kind of softness on his face, there was none to be found. He could as easily have been carved from marble. "You know that, don't you? That's all well and good in the average fairy tale, but this is real life."

"I keep trying to explain to you who I am," Ares said quietly. Almost apologetically, which made every hair on her body feel as if it stood on its end. Because he was the least apologetic creature she had ever met. "I have never been a good prince, it is true, but I'm a prince nonetheless. And we have entered my kingdom, where my word is law. I am afraid that you will discover that I can do as I like."

"But—"

"Call it a fairy tale if you like, *cara mia*," he murmured. "If it helps."

It did not help.

That panic continued to claw at her as the jet landed. As Pia was marched off—escorted, she supposed, and politely, but it all felt rather more kidnap-ish than it had before—and bundled into yet another gleaming car. This time they were driven along a precipitous coastal road that hugged the looming hills on one side and dropped off toward the sea on the other. They skirted around the side of the island, until they came upon what looked to Pia like a perfect fairy-tale castle.

Just in case she didn't already feel as if she'd stumbled into the pages of a storybook already.

It rose as if from a pop-up children's book, blazing with light as it sat up over the sea on a jutting bit of hillside. It even had turrets.

"What is this place?" she managed to ask, half-convinced she was still dreaming.

"It is the Southern Palace, as I said," Ares said from beside her in the car's wide backseat. "If, as I suspect, you are merely pregnant yet not with any child of mine, you will stay here only as long as it takes you to sign the appropriate legal documentation that asserts you have no claim to the throne of my kingdom. And never will."

"I don't want your throne. Or your kingdom."

"Then it will all go very quickly." He turned then, the light from the palace as they approached the first wall beaming into the car and making him gleam. Making him even more beautiful, which was unhelpful. "But if, by some miracle, what you say is true? Then allow me to be the first to welcome you to your new home, Pia. You can expect to be here for some time."

"Once again," she said, working hard to keep her voice calm when she felt nothing but that panic inside her, shredding her, "you might be a prince and this might be your kingdom—"

"There is no *might*, Pia. I am who I say I am."

"Well, *Eric*," she replied, glaring at him, "you cannot actually kidnap women and hold them captive in your palace, no matter who you say you are. I think you'll find it's generally frowned upon."

Ares settled back in his seat as the car slipped into some kind of courtyard, then continued under a grand archway that led deeper beneath the palace. And if he was bothered by the name she'd used—the name he'd given her in New York—he didn't show it.

"You are welcome to register a complaint," he said after a moment, as if he'd taken some time to consider the matter. "In this case, your only recourse would be the king."

And he let out a laugh at that, which was not exactly encouraging.

Still, Pia kept glaring at him. "Is he more reasonable than you? He would have to be, I'd think. You could take me to him right now."

Ares laughed again. "My father is not a safe space," he assured her. "For you, or anyone else."

The car finally came to a stop. And Pia couldn't help the sense of doom that washed over her then. It was that same clawing panic, and something more. Something that made her heart ache.

Ares exited the vehicle with an athletic grace Pia would have preferred not to notice, nodding at the guards who waited there.

Her heart in her throat, Pia followed him, climbing out of the car to find herself in yet another courtyard. She was surrounded on all sides by thick castle walls. Far above was the night sky, riddled with stars. And it had never occurred to her before that there could only really be turrets where there were steep walls all around. That turrets belonged to fortresses, like this one.

But there were no walls steeper and more formidable than the man who stood there, watching her much too intensely as she looked around at her lovely, remote, fairy-tale prison.

Ares. Her prince.

Her jailer.

And whether he was prepared to accept it or not, the man who'd gotten her pregnant.

"I don't want to be here," she told him. But quietly.

"I do not want women wandering about the planet, telling people that I have left them pregnant when I have taken great care never to do such a thing," he replied, almost too easily. "Life does not often give us what we want, Pia."

"If you insist on keeping me here for the moment, I want an exit strategy. I want to know how and when and—"

"If I were you," Ares said, his voice low, "I would be very careful about making any demands."

He moved one finger, and a smartly dressed woman appeared before them as if by magic. "This is Marbella. She will be your chief aide. If you have any questions, you may address them to her."

And he didn't wait for her answer. He simply strode off, princely and remote, his footsteps echoing against the stone until they disappeared.

Pia watched him go, much longer than she should have, and then turned to face the woman who waited at her side.

If she expected a friendly chat, or even a smile, she was disappointed. The other woman bowed slightly, then beckoned Pia to follow her as she set off in a completely different direction into the palace. Each room they passed was more fanciful than the last. Everything was open, airy. Though it was dark, Pia could still sense the ocean all around them. The seething. The whispering. As if it was just there, around the next corner, out of reach—

Marbella led her down a very long corridor that opened up this way and that into galleries and salons, all of them lit up and done in bright, cheerful sort of colors that she imagined did nothing but encourage the sun to linger.

"Who lives here?" she asked after they'd walked a while.

"The Southern Palace has been the preferred retreat of the royal family for centuries, madam," Marbella replied with severe formality. "His Highness is the only member of the family who uses it with any regularity these days, though even he has not been here in some time."

"Does that mean no one else is here?" She thought about what he had said by the car. "Is the king here?"

She thought the other woman stiffened, but that seemed unlikely, given how straight she already stood. "His Majesty resides and remains in the Northern Palace, madam."

Pia nodded sagely, as if she knew the first thing about Atilia, its geography, or its palaces.

Marbella led her on until they reached a beautiful suite of rooms that was to be Pia's for the duration.

Pia did not ask how long that duration was expected to last.

Inside her suite, she found a selection of clothes laid out for her use, that she supposed had to have been flown in from somewhere. She flushed, trying to imagine how Ares had come by the measurements. Had he measured her while she slept? Or did he simply…remember her? And had only added a bit of pregnancy weight to his estimate?

It was amazing how red her face could get at the slightest provocation.

She was grateful when the other woman retreated, leaving her to a glorious set of rooms that she suspected overlooked the water, not that it mattered. A prison was a prison, surely, no matter the view.

Pia took out her phone, was delighted to find she had service, and quickly pulled up what she could find on the kingdom of Atilia. And better still, the Southern Palace.

The palace where she sat was on the southernmost island of the kingdom. What population there was here was spread out across the island in the small villages dotting it. The palace, on the other hand, had been carved out of the side of the mountain as a kind of folly for a long-ago queen. It looked like a fairy-tale castle, but it was, as Pia had felt when she'd looked around, a nearly inviable fortress. There was the Ionian Sea in front and a mountain in back, with only one road in and out.

If anything, she'd been underplaying what was happening here.

The man who had impregnated her was a prince. She

had hardly had time to take that on board. But in case she'd had any doubt, the castle put it to rest. Everything he'd said to her was true.

Ares was a prince. *The* prince. And he had every intention of holding her here.

Until and unless he felt like letting her go.

She was still in her funeral garb when the doctors came, an hour or so later. They'd set up their own makeshift exam room in the palace, and Pia thought about fighting it. Because she, after all, knew what the test was going to say. Surely there had to be a way to keep this from happening. She could refuse to submit herself to the examination...

But she knew without asking, or trying, that there was little point. Ares would keep her here either way until he had his answers. No matter what those answers were.

That runaway train barreled across uneven ground, far off the track, hurtling Pia right along with it.

And the funeral garb felt fitting, really, as she sat in one of the many brightly lit sitting rooms with Ares after the doctors were done with her, awaiting the results.

He stood by one of the open, arched windows that were really doors, looking out at the dark expanse of the ocean. The air this far south was thicker. It insinuated itself against her skin like a caress—but she told herself it was only the humidity. She sat, very primly, on the sofa and tried to keep herself calm.

She *tried*.

The door opened after what seemed like several eternities. Possibly more. All passed in the same tense silence.

Ares turned and the doctor bowed low. "Congratulations, Your Highness," the man said. "You are indeed the father."

Pia couldn't seem to look away from Ares's face. That arrested expression. Something cold and bleak in his gaze.

It made her heart flip over, then sink.

But the doctor wasn't finished. Because of course he wasn't finished. Pia braced herself.

"They are both male," the doctor said.

There was a short, electric pause.

"Both?" Ares asked, his voice a slap.

Neither the doctor nor Ares so much as glanced at Pia, and still she felt as exposed and vulnerable as if she'd been stripped naked and pinned to the wall.

"*Both?*" Ares asked again.

And the words Pia knew were coming sounded to her like bullets when they came, as inevitable and terrible as they'd been when she'd heard them for the first time.

"Yes, Your Highness." The doctor bowed lower. "It is my great honor to inform you that you have been blessed with twins."

CHAPTER SIX

THERE WAS NOTHING but white noise in Ares's head.

A long, sort of flat-line noise that he was fairly certain signaled his own end.

For what else could it be?

Twins.

Twin boys.

He couldn't make the words make any sense. The doctor retreated and Ares stared at Pia as if he could see through that black dress she wore. As if he could see inside of her, where there were *twins*. Boys.

Sons.

Ares's head pounded like a terrible hangover, when he couldn't recall the last time he'd drank to excess. His throat felt dry and scratchy, as if he'd caught a virus and was on the verge of tipping over into misery. He thought it was possible that he shook, too, though he couldn't tell whether that was in him or around him—and he couldn't seem to catch his breath long enough to truly make the determination.

What did it matter what shook? She was carrying twins. His twins. His sons. *His.*

When he finally raised his gaze from her belly and

the impossibility—*two* impossibilities—she carried even now, Pia was still sitting there on the ancient settee that had stood precisely where it was now as long as anyone could remember. Her legs were demurely crossed at the ankles. Her hands were folded neatly in her lap. She gazed back at him, her eyes big and gray and solemn, and fixed on him in a manner that made him…restless.

"Some people might be offended by your reaction," she said quietly, into all that white noise and shake inside him. "But I'm not. My own reaction to the news was very much the same."

"Twins," he managed to say, though his tongue felt tied in knots. "*Twins.*"

She had the grace to look faintly abashed. "You claimed you couldn't have impregnated me with one baby. You were certain. I didn't see what throwing the reality that it was twins into the mix would accomplish."

Ares couldn't argue with that, which made him even more… Whatever he was. He ran a hand over his face, wincing when his palm hit his lip. He'd already forgotten that her older brother had punched him. Matteo, he'd learned on the flight, when he'd finally read the informational one-sheet his aides had prepared for him before the funeral. Matteo Combe, president and CEO of Combe Industries…though the tabloids were having a field day with the punch he'd thrown, even calling him unfit for his own office.

It seemed quaint, almost. A remnant of a former life.

A life where Ares could not possibly have been facing down the fact he'd gotten a woman pregnant. With *twins*.

"Well," Pia said, a bit too brightly. "Perhaps you had better explain to me how you think this imprisonment is going to work."

"How far along are you?" he heard himself ask.

She blinked, then tilted her head slightly to one side.

"I remember you, Pia," Ares retorted, his voice tight. "But I failed to mark that particular night down in my diary."

"Six months," she replied, the lack of inflection in her voice an indictment all its own.

But he was more focused on the span of time. Six months. It made his head swim. And it meant...

"So you will... That is to say, we will..."

He couldn't say the words out loud. Was he sweating?

"In a few months," she said. "But babies are tricky. They do what they like. And I'm told twins tend to come sooner rather than later."

"In the history of this kingdom, there have never been twins."

She dared to look amused. "Ever? Really? In the course of how many thousands of years?"

He thought his growl might have been audible, then. "In the royal family, I should say. There have only ever been single births."

"They say it skips a generation," she offered, helpfully. She studied him for a moment. "My father's aunts were twins."

"Twins," Ares said again.

As if, were he to say the word enough, it would change things, somehow.

Pia stood then, then smoothed out the front of her dress, though it required no smoothing.

"I don't think we're going to have a conversation with much sense in it tonight," she said quietly. Kindly, even, which made him want to…do things. "I suppose that even if you released me on the spot, there would be no leaving here before morning. Why don't we talk about this then. When you've slept on the news and let it settle a bit."

"What do you imagine there is to talk about?" Ares scarcely sounded like himself. "You have… This has…"

"Yes," she said, sounding faintly amused in a way he didn't care for. At all. "You've caught me. I schemed to get pregnant. And to get pregnant with twins, no less. I hunted you down, cold-bloodedly used you to do my evil will, and then, as a coup de grâce, I went away and never contacted you again. Because secretly I knew that my father would drop dead and you would show up at his funeral—"

"I am trying very hard not to blame you for this," Ares told her, and his voice, like the rest of him, was tight and taut and not him at all.

She gave the distinct impression of laughing at him without actually doing so. "That's very kind of you. Because as I recall, we were both there. Unless you'd like to pretend that you, in fact, are a twin and *Eric* is the real father?"

Ares wished that *Eric* was a real person, so he could knock him out.

"I don't understand how this is possible," he said. Possibly not for the first—or fifth—time. "I am a man who enjoys sex, I grant you. But I had no intention of procreating. Ever. I have never been anything less than scrupulous about protection."

She made a sympathetic noise, though she didn't look the least bit sympathetic. "Did you have a vasectomy, then?"

It seemed that Pia was the one delivering knockout blows tonight.

"I did not," Ares said. Stiffly.

"As it turns out, a vasectomy is only 99.9 percent effective. People do still get pregnant after them, though it's rare."

"I've just said I never had one." And he had stopped explaining himself decades ago, yet he felt the strangest urge to leap to his own defense now. "I suppose I might have gotten round to it, eventually."

The fact he'd been so adamantly opposed to procreating and yet hadn't taken steps to ensure he couldn't seemed, now, like the very height of foolishness. What had he been thinking? He had been so certain his blood was poisoned, given the example his father had always set of what happened when their long line of royals met the crown. He had been so clear about the fact he wouldn't risk poisoning any children himself, to end the misery with him. And yet…

"I've had a few months to research protection in a panic, as I, too, failed to understand how this happened," Pia told him in the same calmly informative way that made his teeth grind together. "And as it turns out, as they told us in the convent, the only version of protection that is one hundred percent effective is abstinence."

She even smiled faintly as she said that. And something in Ares turned over, bright with temper.

"Do you think this is entertaining?" he demanded,

his voice hardly more than a growl. "I understand that you didn't plan this. Yet it has happened anyway, apparently. And you have had months to come to terms with it. To make your little jokes about abstinence. But my world ended tonight, Pia."

And he watched, in that sickening mix of dismay and shame, and fury, too, as she slid her hands down over her belly as if she wanted to protect her children.

From him.

Ares shouldn't have cared about something like that.

But it turned out, he did.

"You're not the only person whose world ended today," she threw at him. "In case you've forgotten, you didn't discover this news at a garden party. That was my father's funeral. And thank you for asking, but both of my parents, in fact, were less than thrilled about this. I had the distinct pleasure of telling them that I got pregnant from a tawdry one-night stand with a total stranger. That went over very well. My father called me a tart."

"How can you possibly be a tart if the only man you've ever slept with is me?" Ares asked, and had no idea what that *thing* was that roared about in him. Almost as if he wanted to defend this woman against her own, dead father.

"I think it was the unmarried, pregnant, and no idea who the father was part that got to him," Pia replied. "But then he died a few days later, so I didn't get a chance to follow up on that."

But Ares was still stuck on the fact that she had never touched another man.

Something kicked in him. Something that wasn't

the fact he had *children* coming, like it or not. *Twins.* Something that wasn't all the ramifications of that he couldn't quite face. Not quite yet.

Something that felt a good deal more primitive.

He moved toward her, watching the way her eyes widened. But better still was that little kick of awareness he could see flicker in all that solemn gray.

"No man but me," he said.

"Yes," she said, her voice shakier and much less calm than it had been a moment before. "That is correct."

"You didn't tell me that night."

"Well. You know." Her face was red. Even the tips of her ears were red. "It didn't seem relevant."

He prowled even closer.

"You went to an actual convent. Then a finishing school. And straight after that, you found me in an otherwise forgettable party in Manhattan."

She looked as if she wanted to make a break for it, but stood fast. "That is the sum total of my life thus far, yes. Lucky me."

"I remember you, Pia," he said, his voice low and much too dark, and her eyes widened in response.

But he couldn't seem to help that. Just as he couldn't seem to help himself from reaching out and taking her chin in his hand.

As if she was his.

He expected her to jerk her face away from his hold, but she didn't. And he watched, mesmerized—fascinated— as her pulse went wild in her neck.

Her breathing grew labored. But what intrigued Ares was that he could feel her, inside him. He could feel the kick. The heat. Like touching her was sticking his fingers into an electrical socket, sending sparks showering through him.

"I remember you," he said again, intent and sure, and threaded through with all that electricity. "You flowed over me like water. No hesitation, no concern."

"Perhaps I was significantly drunk," she said, her voice tart, but he could see the softness in her gaze. The melting heat.

"No," he said, remembering. "You were not."

"Perhaps that's what it's always like. I assumed it was. All that..." Her cheeks pinkened even further. "Flowing."

"No," Ares said again, though he sounded too hot, too dark. "That is not what it's like. Not normally."

It had all seemed easy, to his recollection. As if they had been meant to meet like that, then come together in such a glorious, heedless rush. She had arched into his hands as if she'd done it a thousand times before. He'd found her mouth and the place where she was greediest, then tasted both. Her cries had broken over him as if it was a dance they'd practiced a hundred times. More. She had felt explosive in his hands. A glorious, greedy burst of light and sensation.

But more than that, he'd thought when he'd first surged deep inside her and she'd shaken all around him, familiar.

The word that had echoed in his head then was the reason he'd made no effort to seek her out afterward, no matter how often he'd thought of her since.

Home.

Ares, of course, had no home. He'd walked away from his kingdom and had no intention of assuming his throne. Any home he'd had, he'd buried with his mother.

Homes were for other men. Men who deserved them.

Men who were not poisoned with the blood of the Atilian royal family.

He ordered himself to drop his hand. To step back. To put more distance between him and this woman who had shaken him months ago, and here, now, might as well have been a full-scale tsunami.

But he didn't let go the way he knew he should. And instead of stepping back, he moved forward.

"Perhaps we should test it," he said.

"Test what?" She frowned at him. "The last time we tested something I ended up pregnant. With twins."

"Remind me how that happened," he dared her, low and dark.

And it didn't make any sense. He shouldn't want to be anywhere near her, not when his worst nightmare was playing out before him, inside her—

But he couldn't seem to help himself.

Ares bent and pressed his mouth to hers.

And the heat kicked through him, wild and hot. It lit him up, reminding him of that night in Manhattan while it stormed through him, new and mad.

He wasn't satisfied with the press of lips, so he angled his head, taking the kiss deeper. Making it dangerous. Making it clear how easy it had been to go from a conversation at a party to that very long night that had resulted in…this.

He pulled her to him, sliding his hands over her shoulders, then down her back.

And she kissed him back, meeting the thrust of his

tongue. She pressed against him as if she, too, wanted to get closer. Her hands came up and found his chest, and he could feel her belly between them, pushing into him, and that, surely, should have woken him up from the spell—

But instead, Ares kissed her deeper. Harder.

He slid his hands between them and felt the insistent mound of her belly himself.

Her belly. His babies.

And she was the one who wrenched her mouth from his then.

Everything was jumbled around inside of Ares. He had never put his hands on a pregnant woman's belly before. He'd certainly never done so with the knowledge that the babes within were *his*.

It should have disgusted him. He'd always been so revolted at the very idea of fathering a child.

Or maybe it was his own father who had revolted him, now he considered it.

And this was Pia, with her wide eyes, and that generous mouth that drove him crazy. Her taste was in his mouth again, making him wild. Making him hard. Making him feel like someone else entirely.

Someone who put his hands on a woman's belly, understood what he felt there were his own sons—*sons*—and felt a deep, possessive thrill at the notion—

What the hell was happening to him?

All of it was wrong. It was as if he'd been taken over by a different man. A stranger. And yet Ares didn't step away. He didn't even drop his hands. He felt that possessiveness in his chest. His sex.

"I don't think this is the answer to the situation we're

in," Pia said, though her voice wasn't any steadier than he felt. "I think sex has already caused enough trouble, don't you?"

"I don't know that there are any answers," Ares replied. "We might as well console ourselves with the one thing we appear to be so good at."

"I…don't know how to respond to that. I don't have any context."

"Then you'll have to take my word for it." He moved his hands over her bump, telling himself it meant nothing. That he was relearning her shape, that was all. That the fact his palms could not contain her belly, much less the lives within it, didn't matter to him at all. "We are very, very good at it."

And something shifted in him, turning over too fast. Ares found he could no longer tell what, precisely, he meant by that. He was talking about sex, surely. Wasn't he?

But Pia was clearly not inclined to parse the nuances. She stepped back further, almost running into the settee behind her in her haste. And he couldn't deny that there was something in him that took immense satisfaction in the fact that he affected her in this way.

Because no one else had ever touched her. Only him.

That primitive thing inside him, heretofore wholly unknown to him, stirred again.

Her lips were swollen from his kiss. Her body was swollen with not one, but two of his children.

And he might not want to accept what that meant. He might find all of this impossible and bewildering in turn, no matter what the doctor had said. But Ares couldn't deny that the sight of her, lushly fertile and entirely his, made him...

Deeply, darkly triumphant, on a level he hadn't known existed.

"No," she said, very distinctly.

"No?"

"Whatever that look on your face is. Whatever it is, no. I want no part of it."

"But all bets are off now, are they not?" He felt...ferocious. "I am a man who never planned to have children, yet you are carrying two, and they are mine. Who knows what else we think we cannot have, or do not want, that will happen here against our will?"

"I have no intention of spending the next few months trapped here," she told him, in that same sober, serious way. "You now know that you're the father of these babies. *My* babies. I'm glad. That wasn't a secret I meant to keep from you in the first place. But now that you know, there's no need for all these..." She looked around the room, and waved her hand as if to take it all in, and the whole of the palace besides. "All these royal shenanigans."

Ares had never felt the weight of the Atilian crown more than he did in the moment she dismissed it, and so easily.

"Here's the problem, Pia," he said, feeling as growly and uneven as he sounded. "I cannot decide what to do with you."

"I don't recall signing myself over into your care. You don't decide what happens to me. I do."

"You are a quandary," he told her, and the things that roared inside him were loud again. They competed with each other. They were made of furor and fang, and over and over again, they drew blood. That damned blood of his. "I have to decide how to proceed."

"Terrific. You go ahead and think on that to your heart's content. Meanwhile, I'll fly straight back to England and carry on with my life, shall I?"

"That's not going to happen." When she scowled at him, he laughed. Because what was there to do but laugh at the very notion that either one of them could wander back to their normal lives now? Or ever? "I think perhaps, *cara*, it is not I who am being unreasonable."

"Says the man who kidnapped me."

"You say you wish to go back to England. Where would you go?"

Pia's frown deepened. "Home. Obviously."

"The paparazzi already have their teeth in this story. Your brother is fielding calls for his resignation after his display of violence and I'm certain that the palace will already have received a thousand queries about whether or not his pregnant sister is the reason he belted me. Do you think they'll magically leave you alone?"

"They always have before," she said, and for the first time, he understood how very sheltered she'd been. It should have appalled him, surely. But instead, he had the strangest urge to shelter her.

"Convents and finishing schools do not capture the public's imagination the way a scandal does," he told her. "Or the world would be a very different place."

"We can still deny it." She sounded almost…desperate. "Matteo is a Combe. Combes are always punching people. What's a prince in the mix?"

"I think you know better."

"I don't see why anyone has to know about this if we don't tell them," she argued. "It's always seemed to me that the people the tabloids hound the most are the ones who court the attention. If we don't court it, surely they'll move on to something else."

"Pia. Remember, please, that I am not some debutante's gelded date, on hand to waltz on command at her coming-out ball. I am the Crown Prince of this kingdom, for my sins. The very hint that any woman's baby could be mine will send my people into a frenzy."

She shook her head, her face pale again. "What does that matter? You told me that you don't want children and don't want a wife. Frenzy or not."

"I don't."

"So there's no point to any of these conversations, is there?"

"What I want and what I plan to do with what has happened are two different things, I think," he said.

He wasn't sure why her reluctance made his temper kick at him. Only that it did.

And he stared her down until she lowered her eyes, there in the palace his ancestors had built while the blue blood he hated—and yet shared with all those who had stood here before him—stormed in his veins.

It made him feel alive, like it or not. It made him *want*.

It made him wonder how this was going to end.

"If I were you," Ares told her, all princely command, "I would resign myself to it."

CHAPTER SEVEN

PIA HAD NO INTENTION of resigning herself to anything, thank you, and especially not her own kidnapping.

Sure, she'd gotten into his car and onto his plane of her own free will. It had seemed vastly preferable to the baying press outside Combe Manor. But she hadn't expected to come here. That had to count against him. She was determined it did.

She broke away from that room where she'd felt as if Ares was holding her in his grip, where her mouth still throbbed from his kisses—God help her, that man could *kiss*—and hurtled herself out into the palace corridors. It took her longer than it should have to find her way back to her suite, and by the time she made it she was tired, emotional, and shaking.

Pia told herself she was peckish, that was all. Because once the morning sickness had stopped, she'd become ravenous. And hadn't stopped.

Her aide met her inside her rooms and quickly produced a lavish spread for Pia to choose from. And she wanted so desperately to be the sort of unwilling captive who could turn up her nose at anything she was offered. Not to mention, weren't there too many tales about unwary virgins who were lured into treacherous places they could have left—if only they hadn't eaten there?

"Lucky that you're no virgin, then," she muttered to herself as she helped herself to a heaping plate of seconds.

But after the palace staff had swept all evidence of her private feast away, Pia stayed where she was. She sat up straight in the most uncomfortable chair in her outermost sitting room. She channeled her many years of being taught manners by unimpressed nuns, sat so she wouldn't drift off to sleep, and waited.

The hours ticked past. The night wore on.

And when she decided it was late enough that even infamous playboy princes—not that she'd worn down her phone battery by Googling him exhaustively—had taken themselves off to bed, if only because there was precious little other entertainment to be had here on the southern tip of the middle of nowhere, she stood. She stretched her protesting limbs, let herself out of her room again, and resolved that she would walk out of this palace if necessary.

It took her a while to find her way through the maze of halls and corridors again, and she got lost more than once. But eventually she found herself on the ground level, where she set about looking for a door that led outside—instead of into yet another courtyard.

Unfortunately, there were courtyards everywhere, as if every member of the royal family who'd ever spent time here had built their own.

There were courtyards that opened up to the sky and others that were really more like squares beneath the floor above. There were courtyards that opened into the sea itself, but Pia couldn't seem to find one that led to that road she knew they had taken in. She kept getting turned around. She thought she was retracing her steps when she turned a corner and yelped because someone was *right there*.

"Imagine my surprise," Ares said darkly, "to be roused from my slumber by my staff, and told that the palace was not under attack, but that one of my guests—my only guest—was creeping about the place like a criminal."

"I'm not creeping anywhere and I'm certainly not a criminal," Pia threw at him.

And only then did she take in what he was wearing.

Or more to the point, *not* wearing.

Because the Crown Prince of Atilia stood there before her wearing nothing but a pair of loose black trousers, slung low on his hips as if to suggest that he had been sleeping naked and had tossed them on when he came to find her.

And everything else was just…him.

Those wide, smoothly muscled shoulders. That broad chest that narrowed to lean hips. Ares kept himself in excellent physical condition—she hadn't built that up in her fantasies since New York, it turned out—all rangy muscles and that loose-limbed elegance he wore so easily.

He wasn't the only one who remembered that night in Manhattan. She did, too. How she had crawled over him in sheer, greedy delight. How she had tasted him, tempting them both nearly past endurance. How she had filled her mouth with salt and man and the dark heat that rose between them still.

Here. Now.

"Why aren't you dressed?"

She all but shrieked out the question, half in a gasp, and knew even as it escaped her lips that she'd revealed herself. That she'd given herself away.

Completely.

"Why, pray, would I be dressed?" he asked mildly, though his green eyes glittered there, in the deserted hall. "Perhaps you have not noticed, Pia, but it is the middle of the night. Why are you still dressed as you were hours before? And more to the point, why are you lurking about as if you are casing the place? Are you?"

Pia didn't know what came over her. One moment, she'd had a clear sense of purpose. Of direction. Or intention, anyway, no matter if she couldn't quite find her way.

And then in the next, Ares was standing before her half-dressed. And she was still trapped here in this fairy-tale fortress. And she was an orphan and a mother, both at the same time. And all of that seemed to crash into her.

As if that damned runaway train had looped around and plowed straight into her, flattening her.

Her face crumpled, no matter how hard she fought to keep it smooth. Unbothered. And as she fought off the huge sob that seemed to roll out of her, then on top of her like a great weight, she saw Ares's expression... change.

Pia kept thinking that she'd reached the absolute outer limit of the shame that any one person could feel. She kept thinking there could be no further depths to plumb.

And then something else happened.

She tried to cover her face, because she couldn't stand the fact that he was *right there*, watching her as she quite literally fell apart in front of him.

But his hands were on her, brushing her shoulders and then shifting. Before she knew what was happening he was lifting her up, hauling her high against his chest.

"Don't be foolish," she sobbed at him, her hands still over her face. "I'm hugely pregnant. You'll give yourself a hernia."

"Pia," Ares said in the most regal voice she'd heard from him yet. "Please be so good as to shut up."

She obeyed him. Or she tried, anyway, but she couldn't keep the sobs inside. And later she would find herself appalled and humiliated that she'd so easily surrendered. To her emotions, to him. To everything. But here, now, she tipped her head forward, rested against his shoulder, and let the tears come.

Later she would regret this, she was sure of it.

But for a while, there was only the width and strength of his shoulder, holding her steady as he moved. There was the scent of him, clean and male, with a hint of something else. Soap, perhaps. Cologne, maybe. She couldn't quite tell, but she knew that scent. She remembered it. And it soothed her.

She didn't understand why he should be capable of calming her when no one else ever had. When her life was filled, in fact, with people and places and things that did the exact opposite of calming her. But she didn't have it in her, just then, to fight him.

Not when he was so strong, and so warm, and when

his arms wrapped around her as if she was light and sweet and beautiful. As if he could carry her forever, and would.

And when he finally set her down again, she had to bite her own tongue to keep from protesting.

She wiped at her face, then looked around, and it took her longer than it should have to recognize that she was in a bathroom. A huge, suitably palatial bathroom, that was. If she wasn't mistaken, he had taken her back to her own rooms.

And she sat there, feeling limp and fragile with the force of her own feelings—none of which she could name—as the Crown Prince of Atilia filled her bath. She sat where he'd put her, there on the wide lip of the oversize tub. And she watched him, vaguely astonished that His Royal Highness knew how to go about such a mundane task.

The beauty of her convent education was that she and the rest of the girls from wealthy families who could afford to go there had been taught how to function like regular people. It was one of the convent's primary missions, in fact.

"You do realize I have servants to do this, don't you?" one of the girls in Pia's year had thrown at Mother Superior one morning as they'd all been scrubbing the floors of their dormitory.

"My dear child," Mother Superior had replied, in that mild voice that made them all wince, "you are being taught basic chores not for you, though you can certainly benefit from learning them, but for those servants. In the perhaps vain notion that a dose of empathy might allow you to inhabit your place in this world with more consideration for others."

That had stuck with Pia, along with the punishment Mother Superior had levied against their entire class for the rest of the semester—that was, scrubbing the whole of the great hall. On their hands and knees.

Now she sat in a palace with a man she barely knew but would have sworn didn't lift a single finger if someone else could do it for him. A prince who'd given her twins and spirited her away from her life—twice, now. And she wondered who'd taught him the same lesson.

And then wondered what was wrong with her that she wanted, so desperately, to believe that he was capable of something like empathy. Because that might make him into the father she knew he didn't want to become.

Why do you want him to be a father? she asked herself, harshly enough that she could have been one of her own parents. *You can raise these babies perfectly well on your own. You don't need him.*

That was true. She knew that was true. And still, Pia watched Ares sprinkle bath salts over the hot water as if this was church. Then she didn't know what to feel when he came back to her, there on the edge of the tub set in an alcove with the sea outside.

"I think it is time you took off this shroud you are wearing, *cara mia*," he said in a low voice.

Pia looked down. She knew she hadn't changed her clothes, but she hadn't really processed the fact that she was still wearing that same black dress, severe and solemn and not remotely comfortable, that she'd worn to her father's funeral. And then to his grave.

She raised her gaze to Ares. "I don't think I want to."

Something moved over his face. He crouched down before her so he was on eye level with her. His arms were on either side of her legs, caging her there against the tub, and she thought that on some level, she should hate her heart for the way it beat so hard when he was close. She really should.

Ares shifted, moving back on his heels, but he did not rise. And his eyes were green and gold and that, too, felt like betrayal.

"I understand," he said, astonishing her anew.

Pia wanted to believe that, too. With a fervor that boded ill for her.

A faint smile moved over his mouth as he saw her expression. "When my mother died she lay in state, as is the custom here. And then my father and I walked through the streets as we transported her to her final resting place. I wore the typical regalia of my station, a uniform I have never found comfortable in the least. And yet, when it was over, when I was out of the public eye and back in my private rooms, I found I couldn't bear to move. I couldn't bear to change out of that uniform." His gaze seemed particularly green then. "Because I knew that doing so would indicate that I was moving on in some way."

"You loved your mother very much."

"I did. Did you not love your father? Or your own mother?"

He moved a hand to rest it on her thigh, and Pia was…astounded. She could feel the heat of him, all that power and strength, and be aware of him as a man. But she could also find that grip of his comforting, apparently.

She felt too many things to choose one, much less name it.

"There is no right answer," Ares said. "I had an excellent relationship with my mother. I have no relationship with my father. Parents are complicated."

And Pia was sure she wasn't the only one of them who was painfully aware that they were soon to be parents themselves. That they could inflict God knew what on their own children.

It was an unbearable intimacy to share with a man who was as good as a stranger.

"My parents had children only as an afterthought," she heard herself blurt out.

Anything to stop thinking about herself and Ares as terrible parents. Or any kind of parents.

What she'd said was true, of course. She'd read articles that had said as much, and less nicely. But she had never said it out loud herself before. And in a way, it felt like grief to hear her own voice, speaking that truth.

But somehow, she wanted to keep going. "Or at least, *I* was an afterthought. I suppose they always planned to have my brother. The heir of my father's dynastic dreams, et cetera."

She stared down at Ares's hand, and wanted to slide her own on top of his more than she wanted to breathe. She would never know how she kept her hands to herself. Or how she pushed on when she wasn't sure how or why she was speaking in the first place.

"When they focused on me at all, I think they saw me as a project," she told Ares as the scent of the lavender bath salts filled the room. "I don't honestly know that they were capable of loving anything but one another. I don't mean that in a bad way. I loved them both, I think. But it was always bound up in the ways I disappointed them."

His green eyes were grave. "How could you possibly be a disappointment?"

Pia didn't know how to answer him. And she knew that the reason for that was ego, nothing more. Pride. She didn't want to tell this man what he should have been able to see with his own two eyes.

And would, now. Now that he knew who she was. And therefore knew who her mother was. It was one thing to be herself, Pia knew. She could do that. It was when she was compared to Alexandrina that people felt the most let down.

Her parents most of all.

But she couldn't bring herself to point that out to Ares. She didn't have it in her.

"I'm glad I'm having boys," she said instead. "I think that must be easier."

Whatever light she'd seen in his gaze shuttered then. He moved his hand, which struck Pia as yet another tragedy she was unprepared to face, and reached into the water behind her.

He tested the temperature, then moved back, rising to his feet in a lithe rush that was nothing short of dazzling, with all that muscle and grace.

"You should get in," he told her, sounding distant and royal again. "Then I suggest you get some sleep. I cannot promise you that grief goes anywhere, but the sooner you start the process of moving on, the sooner you'll get to the part that's easier. Eventually, you'll find it hurts a lot less than it did."

"I think that must feel like losing them all over again," Pia said, without thinking.

Ares's gaze was too hot, too arrested as it snapped to hers.

"It does," he bit out.

And he left her there, sitting in her funeral dress on the side of a hot bath, wondering how and why he'd made drawing her bath feel like a gift. And why she wanted nothing more than to sink into it, fully clothed, and lie there until she stopped *feeling*.

When she stood, she felt unsteady on her feet. She found herself crying all over again as she pulled the dress off, then folded it neatly, placing it much too carefully on one of the nearby counters.

As if it was precious to her when really, she wanted to burn it. She had worn it twice in six weeks' time. She would never wear it again.

And when she sank down in the bath, and lost herself in the silken embrace of hot water, lavender, and steam, she let the tears fall until they stopped of their own volition. Pia didn't know who she cried for. The mother who had never loved her the way Pia had wished so desperately she would. The father who had viewed her as something to barter, or an amusement, but never a real person.

Or this new life she'd stumbled into, whether she wanted it or not. The babies she carried, the prince who had fathered them, and the terrifying, unknown future that loomed ahead of them all.

She cried herself dry, and only then did she rise up from the tub, towel herself off, and take herself into the vast, airy confection of a four-poster bed that waited in the bedroom. She crawled into the center of the bed, turned over onto her side to find the only position where she could be remotely comfortable, and wrapped one arm around her belly.

"I promise you this," she murmured out loud to the twin lives inside of her. "I will never barter you away. I will tell you I love you every single day of your lives. And you will never, ever find yourself wondering on the day of my death if you grieve because you miss me—or because you don't."

And still murmuring vows to the sons she would bear within a few short months, but treat better if it killed her, Pia finally fell asleep.

CHAPTER EIGHT

ARES HAD NO IDEA what was happening to him as each day bled into the next, then a week slipped by. Then another.

And he and Pia stayed suspended in the same waiting game.

It was easy enough to make the Southern Palace his base of operations. So easy, in fact, that he couldn't quite remember why it had been so important to him to live apart from Atilia in the first place.

He flew in and out, from one royal engagement to another. And despite the barrage of scandalmongering headlines about him and Matteo Combe—and the expectant state of the Combe heiress the world had ignored until the funeral—his actual life was the same as it had been before. Did it matter what he called his base when he flew everywhere anyway?

Ares assured himself that nothing had changed. Nothing but his location.

Except he noticed that he found himself almost eager to return to the palace at the end of each engagement.

Almost as if he couldn't truly be easy until he'd seen Pia again.

If she had cried again after that first night, she never showed it. Nor did she make further attempts to break out of the castle, which was a relief if only because it prevented Ares from sharing parts of himself when he never, ever did such things.

The reports Ares received about her in his absence were always glowing. She was unfailingly polite and kind to all members of the staff. She went on walks, around and around the many courtyards, and at low tide, down to the beach, where she was known to spend time on the rocks, staring out toward the horizon. She never tried to lose her security detail. She seemed perfectly happy to have regular checkups with the doctor.

Her only request had been a laptop computer, which Ares had been more than happy to provide, particularly as it gave him leave to monitor what she did.

After all, he had never promised her privacy.

And that was how he discovered that what Pia did with her time was write an online column for one of those internet magazines that Ares had always personally believed were the scourge of the earth. He found this discovery so astounding that he sat with it for nearly a full week before it occurred to him to do anything about it.

One night, after he'd flown back from some or other formal charity event in mainland Europe, he found her curled up in what the staff had informed him was her favorite room of the palace. It was known as the Queen's Sitting Room, in the ancient wing, and had been built to accommodate a queen who had loved the ocean, her books and needlework, and liked to sit where she could look out all day while the business of the court carried on elsewhere. During the day the light cascaded in through the arched windows. At night, light made to look like candles blazed from every surface while the waves surged against the rocks outside.

Ares moved soundlessly into the room, not sure what to do with the wall of sensation and something perilously close to longing that slammed into him the moment he saw her.

Every moment he saw her, if he was honest.

Pia sat cross-legged on the chaise pointed toward the windows, a pillow over her lap—or what lap she had, with her huge, pregnant belly in the way. She was frowning down as she typed, worrying her bottom lip between her teeth, and Ares was only a man.

And it had been a long time indeed since he had taken a woman, now that he thought about it. Too long. Months.

Ares found he didn't actually want to scour his memory, because he was terribly afraid that Pia really had haunted him. That he might not have touched another woman since that night in New York.

He didn't want to consider that possibility, so he considered her instead.

His gaze traced the elegant line of Pia's neck, and the little wisps of dark hair that had tumbled down from the knot at the top of her head. He leaned against the doorjamb, letting his gaze drift lower. Her breasts swelled against the loose top she wore and he remembered covering them with his hands in New York. Now he wondered if they would spill over from his palms, so generous had they become. His mouth watered.

And there was something about her lush, swollen

belly that got to him, no matter how he tried to pretend otherwise.

There was something about the fact that she carried his babies, that she was big and round by his doing, that made something dark and primitive wind around and around inside him until he was tight like a coil.

He didn't know how he felt about becoming a father, but that had nothing to do with his appreciation of what he had done to her body. Or how she seemed to take to it so easily, so naturally, like one of the ancient goddesses that the locals claimed had first lived here on the site where the palace stood.

He shook himself, bemused at the direction of his own thoughts.

"When did you become an advice columnist?" he asked her, unaware until he spoke that his voice had gone all…gravelly.

But he couldn't worry about that when he had the distinct pleasure of watching Pia jolt in surprise. She whipped her head around, and then Ares's pleasure turned to a deeper joy as her cheeks reddened.

The way they always did when she saw him.

As if she couldn't keep herself from flushing pink and deeper red, which made him wonder if she was pink and red all over.

The possibilities made him ache.

"How do you…?" she began.

But her voice trailed off. She looked down at the laptop before her, and Ares braced himself for her temper. For the outburst that was almost surely coming.

He had to wonder if he'd asked the question specifically to provoke her.

If he'd lowered himself to such games.

But when Pia looked at Ares again, her gray gaze was resigned. "You're monitoring this laptop. Of course you are. I don't know why I didn't assume you were from the start."

Ares inclined his head slightly. "For security purposes, naturally. This is a royal palace."

"And because you're nosy." Her gaze stayed steady. "You want to know things about me without having to ask."

He could see that moment shimmer between them, Pia in her funeral dress on the side of that tub and him too close and much too open, and he was sure she could, too. But she didn't say anything.

"You could be in league with the tabloid reporters who swarmed us in Yorkshire," Ares said mildly instead. "You could have been planted by my enemies."

"Do you actually have enemies?" Pia asked, her voice even more mild than his. It scraped at him. "Or is this a part of those many wars you appear to be waging, though no one is waging them back at you?"

Ares leaned one shoulder against the doorjamb, crossed his arms, and regarded her sternly. "I suppose you could say I am my own war."

He certainly hadn't meant to say that. He didn't even know where the words had come from. Only that once they were out there, he couldn't deny the stark truth of them.

Or the acrid taste they left behind in his mouth.

It was like the first night she'd been here and that bizarre urge he'd had to *tend to her*. Ares wasn't certain he had *tended to* another person in the whole of his life, save his own mother in her final days. He hardly knew her. He knew the urge even less. It felt as if he'd been hit on the head and had only come to—and back into himself—when she'd reminded him of the fact that she was having sons.

His sons.

Every time he thought less of the sweet ripeness of her body and more about what that ripeness would result in, it hit him in the same way. Hard. Debilitating.

A full-on body blow.

"If you are your own war, you are lucky, Ares. That means you can call it off at any time." She closed the laptop and set it aside, her gray gaze on him. "You can have an armistice whenever you like."

"It is not quite that easy."

But he sounded more uncertain of that than he should have.

"Why are you spying on me?" she asked him, direct and to the point, that gaze still firm on his.

And if her voice had been sharp, or accusing, Ares would have known what to do. He could have handled it with a dose of royal arrogance, or that edgy thing in him that was always too close to the surface when he was in Atilia. Or near her.

Instead, he felt something like...outgunned.

"I would not call it spying," he replied, after a moment, but the words didn't seem to fit right in his mouth. "I told you. There were security concerns."

"Yes," she said, lifting up that chin of hers again. "I write a column. It's silly, really. There are lots of people who go through life without having to suffer through a finishing school. After all, its only real purpose is to make a person—and let's not kid ourselves, it's always a female person—so scrupulously well mannered that she could be a queen, if necessary."

Something powerful seemed to roar between them at that.

But Ares refused to acknowledge it. And Pia's cheeks only got redder.

"Hypothetically speaking, of course," she hurried to say. She looked away then, and Ares wondered if he was reddening, too, deep inside. "There's that story of the Queen of England at some dinner party. They'd set out finger bowls and the guest of honor picked his up and drank from it, which ought to have humiliated him. And would have, if he'd known. Everyone froze, not sure what to do in the face of such a breach of etiquette. But what did the queen do? She reached over, picked up her own finger bowl, and downed it like a shot. I don't know if that's true, but I like to think it is."

"Because you like to advise your readers to drink the contents of the finger bowls they encounter?" Ares asked. Darkly.

He felt…not himself, already. But even more so when Pia only gazed at him so calmly that he felt as if he'd turned into some kind of beast where he stood, misshapen and overlarge.

"Figuratively speaking," she replied. "I pretend to talk about good manners in my column. But really what I'm talking about is how to be kind."

"Kindness is overrated," Ares heard himself growl.

But Pia only shook her head. "No. It's really not."

"I admire these lofty sentiments, I do," Ares said in that same dark tone, all beast and very little prince. "But if you know that I have been monitoring what you do on that laptop, you must also know that I'm aware you monetize those columns of yours."

If he expected that to get to her, he was disappointed when all she did was smile. Patiently. In a manner that made him want to…break things.

Or get his hands on all that round, tempting lushness.

"No one knows it's me, do they?" That smile of hers was so bland it bordered on offensive. "I can assure you, no one wants to hear from poor little rich girl Pia Combe about how to be a better person."

"You have been writing this column for years. Since your second year of university, if my math is correct." He knew that it was.

"Well, there's only so much finishing a girl can do," Pia said lightly. Airily. She didn't actually wave her hand through the air dismissively, but it felt as if she had. "I thought it was a more reasonable outlet than some of the other ones my friends took up. Unsuitable men, for example. Or tempting scandal and often fate itself in all sorts of disreputable nightclubs. Unfortunate substances. A little column I never expected anyone to read seemed rather tame in comparison, but then, I have always been the little brown sparrow in a family of nothing but brightly plumed parrots. It felt very me."

Ares scowled at her. "I have absolutely no idea why you are suddenly talking about birds. Much less *plumage*."

"I know who I am. That's all I'm saying."

"You certainly don't need the money," Ares said, as if he'd caught her involved in some kind of con.

"I don't keep the money," she said, making a face as

if he was the one drinking out of finger bowls at formal banquets. "It's not a lot, or not by the standards I imagine you're used to, but I give it away. There are always needy people trying to raise money for various causes, and I like to give where I can. Without any strings."

"You could do that with the interest off a single month of your trust fund, one assumes."

"I could. But I was raised by Eddie Combe, who liked to rant and rave about the value of an honest day's work. I'm not pretending to work in any mines, but there's something to be said about earning my own money and spending it how I like." Her gaze searched his. "In fairness, I suppose crown princes aren't generally encouraged to do such things."

"There are some kingdoms that exult in the sight of their royals getting dirty with the common folk, but Atilia is not one of them," Ares said. "My mother spent time in the Royal Hospital, but ministering to the ill was about as far as the country was willing to let her go."

Thinking of his mother didn't bring the stab of grief it normally did. Possibly because he kept thinking that his mother would have loved Pia unreservedly. Ares could almost see them together, sitting in this very room, passing that laptop back and forth and discussing who next to help.

He found he was clenching his jaw so hard he was surprised he didn't snap a tooth.

"If you can help, you should," Pia said quietly, so much an echo of his childhood that Ares had to blink to make certain he wasn't sitting with his mother again, letting her quiet goodness cancel out his father's latest tantrum.

"I had no idea when I met you in New York that you were such a saint," he heard himself growl then.

Pia blinked, then flushed a deeper shade of red, and he felt as if he'd slapped her. That made him feel monstrous again. A cartoon beast, all fur and fury.

But he couldn't seem to stop himself from making every one of these moments with her…worse.

"Did you not?" she asked, lightly enough, though her gaze had gone cool. Wary. "I felt certain I was wearing my halo."

"I don't recall you wearing anything at all."

And that electric thing was back, bright and hot between them. Ares could feel his pulse thick and hot in his temples. In his chest.

In his greedy, hungry sex.

"I sit here every day," she said, though her voice was scratchier than it had been a moment before and there was a light in her eyes that made his pulse…worse. He decided to take that as a kind of victory. "I read a lot of tabloid takedowns. Alternate reality versions of me. Versions where I cold-bloodedly trapped a prince with my uterus. Then pitted said prince against my own brother, using my unborn child as collateral. I spend a lot of time wondering how it's possible that a person who never appeared in a single scandalous story before, ever, could attract the hatred of so many so fast."

"Is this about to veer into sparrows and parrots again?"

"I already feel stripped naked, is what I'm trying to tell you." Pia swallowed, hard. "It's bad enough that every time I pick up my phone or open a search engine I'm treated to more side-by-side comparisons between me and my mother, who, you may have heard, is still widely held to be the most beautiful woman who ever lived. I don't need you to come in here and taunt me."

"Taunt you?"

Ares hadn't expected that. Just as he didn't see it coming when Pia rose to her feet, betraying a gracefulness he felt certain she didn't know she possessed—but he could feel. All over him like a caress. She picked up the laptop and clutched it to her chest, then looked at him as if he was still very much that cartoon monster.

"I don't know what you want from me," she said, so quietly that it felt like condemnation. As if she could see the poison in his blood from where she stood. "I don't think you know either, which is the only reason why I'm tolerating this."

"This palace, renowned the world over for its beauty and never made available to the public. A life of ease, waited upon hand and foot. This is what you feel you must 'tolerate.'"

"You didn't liberate me from a gutter," Pia said, in that same quiet, deliberate way. "I'm not dazzled by your material possessions. I can see quite clearly that this is a prison no matter how lovely the furnishings might be."

What Ares didn't understand was why he felt as if he was in prison, too, when he was the one who came and went as he pleased.

"Consider this a grace period," she told him, very much as if she was the one with the control here. "I had months to get used to the fact that I was pregnant with twins. It wouldn't be fair of me not to accord you the same span of time to come around to the notion. But the clock is ticking, Ares. You can't keep me here forever and even if you could, there will soon be three of us."

"I would not challenge me if I were you." And his voice was a dark ribbon of sound he hardly recognized.

"You will have to make a decision," Pia replied as if she couldn't see the threat in him. Or didn't care. "Or do you think that I will have these babies locked away here, and then raise them like this, isolated from the world? As if we don't exist? You may be ashamed of them. Of me. But I am not."

"I never said I was ashamed."

She drew herself up, which only made him more aware of her lushness.

"Your indecision might keep me here," she said, as if she hadn't heard him. "I might even like it, as it keeps me from having to have unpleasant conversations with my older brother and everyone else who is suddenly dying to know my personal business."

She moved toward him then, the laptop in one arm and the other one wrapped over her belly.

"Pia—" he began, as if her name in his mouth didn't remind him too much of her taste. As if he didn't *ache*.

"But you will not lock these babies away from the world, Ares. They will not be victims to your indecision. Do you understand me?" And he had never seen that expression on her face before. Fierce. Sure. *Maternal*, something in him whispered. "My children will walk in the sun. They will be loved. They will not be hidden away like someone's dirty secret, and I don't care if it is in a palace. I won't have it."

And he wanted to stop her. He wanted to somehow

talk his way through the great mess inside of him, but he found himself frozen solid.

Unable to do anything but stand there, more monster than man.

And Ares wasn't sure that ratio was moving in his favor as she swept past him and disappeared down the hall.

Leaving him to feel the true weight of this palace he'd made a prison, as surely as if he'd fitted it with bars.

Ares had learned a long time ago not to read tabloid interpretations of his life, but he still found himself flipping idly through the worst of them on his tablet the next day as he flew to the Northern Island for the grand dedication of something or other.

A bank, perhaps. A monument.

He didn't care about that. Because the tabloids were filled with base speculation and nasty insinuation. Nothing new, but Ares found it clawed at him in a whole new way when the subject was Pia instead of him.

His own face was everywhere, with shots of him laid out on the ground and the bloody lip Matteo Combe had given him.

Matteo had been taken to task by his own Board of Directors, who were muttering about a no-confidence vote. They'd even gone so far as to sic an anger management specialist on him for a time, which Ares couldn't help but find amusing.

But there was nothing amusing about the things they almost but not quite called Pia. Because instead of fading away with nothing new to add to the story, it seemed the tabloids had only gotten bolder in their coverage during the time he and Pia had been in the Southern Palace.

Playboy Prince's pregnancy scandal! the headlines screamed.

Ares supposed he should count himself lucky that no one had dared mention the tabloids to his face.

He was congratulating himself on that as he stood in the grand, marble lobby of the Royal Bank of Atilia that was being dedicated to the King, where he was meant to say a few words. But there was a change in the crowd, suddenly, as he prepared himself to speak. He could feel it in the air. The ripple effect. The whispering and the gasping, followed by deep bows and curtsies all around.

Ares swore beneath his breath.

But he knew that he betrayed not a single emotion on his face when his father came in all his considerable state to stand beside him. Ares turned, as was required, and performed his own bow to his monarch.

"Prince Ares," the King said by way of greeting, and only because people were watching and would likely expect him to greet his only son.

"I did not expect to see you here, Your Majesty," Ares said beneath his breath as they stood for a rousing go at the Atilian national anthem. And he should not have seen his father, because it was well-known amongst the palace staff that the crown prince and the king preferred never to be in each other's company. "My secretary must have made a mistake."

"There was a mistake, all right," King Damascus retorted, making no attempt to hide his glare and no matter that the crowd was on the "*long may our king in grace and wisdom preside*" part of the song. "It's about time you and I have a word."

Ares could think of very little he would like less.

But they were in public. There was the brief ceremony to get through, made ten times worse by the presence of his father and all the extra pomp and circumstance that went along with the presence of the King of Atilia at such a banal event. And when it was done, he had no choice but to exit several steps behind his father as custom dictated, then follow him as commanded.

Because a son could rebel against his father. But Ares's father was also his king, and what the king decreed was law.

The old man insisted that they return to the Northern Palace, where Ares had made it a point not to set foot since his mother had died.

He knew his father was well aware of this.

But King Damascus wanted to draw it out, because he was as sadistic now as he had ever been. He marched Ares straight back to that private sitting room of his, where he had been lecturing Ares in between bouts of temper for as long as Ares could remember.

This time, Ares took the seat his father indicated and lounged in it. Not insolent, necessarily, but not reverent, either.

"This feels nostalgic," he said after the silence had dragged on too long.

"I'm glad you think so," the king said. "I feel nauseated, myself."

Ares smiled. Thinly. "Shall I contact your staff, sir? Do you require medical attention?"

The king moved to his personal bar, and Ares watched with a certain sense of resignation as his father poured himself a drink from yet another crystal decanter that Ares imagined would soon be in broken shards all over the stone floor. He did not offer Ares a drink, because he was still as petty as ever.

"Do you want to explain to me why your pregnant little piece is all over every paper?" the king demanded.

Ares wasn't sure what, precisely, it was that surged in him then. But he knew it was violent. Dark and furious, and aimed at his father.

Which he knew was treason.

But he didn't care.

"I beg your pardon, Your Majesty," he said icily. "You must surely be referring to yourself. I have no 'piece,' as you put it."

"You told me this would never happen," his father snarled at him. "You *promised* me, or I would have married you off years ago."

"Nature will do what it will do, father," Ares said, with a great flippancy he in no way felt about Pia or the babies she carried. "I don't understand your concern. I am not married. There is no actual scandal, there are only tabloids making noise."

"Was it noise that knocked you flat?"

Ares made himself stay where he was, seated and unthreatening. "That was a misunderstanding, nothing more."

"Do not expect my permission to marry her," his father said, and though he grew smaller and more wizened every time Ares saw him, that glare of his was as baleful as ever. "Do not think that the fact she is a

San Giacomo in any way makes up for all that peasant blood in her."

"I will remind you, sire," Ares said, acidly, "that I do not require your permission to marry. You struck down that law yourself, the better to make way for your own mistress."

"You mean your queen," his father growled. "Her Majesty Queen Caprice to the likes of you, and I warn you, I will tolerate no disrespect."

Ares forced himself to lounge back in his chair, though he wanted to be the one to start breaking things, this time. "And what of our great and glorious Queen Caprice? My understanding was that her chief attraction was her supposed fertility. Yet I've seen no sign that she is expecting your heirs."

"Watch yourself, boy."

"One is tempted to conclude that the reason you sired but one disappointing child was your fault. Not my mother's, as has been commonly agreed."

He meant: *by you and your doctors.*

"Is that your goal? You think that if you start having illegitimate children it will make you the better man?" His father laughed, but in that angry way of his that allowed for no actual humor. "On the contrary, Ares, all it does is remind the kingdom what a waste of space you are. A profligate playboy, governed by his base appetites. I should thank you for doing me a favor."

Ares stared back at this man that he had feared and hated for most of his life. Here in this room, where he had been threatened, belittled, and shouted at more times than he could count. Here where he had made decisions based entirely on how not to be the man facing him.

And he could cite chapter and verse about the things he didn't want. The man he didn't wish to become. The blood in him he hated, that had run hot just now, so desperately did he want to respond to the sneering violence in his father's voice in kind.

But he had other weapons.

You are always in a war, Pia had said.

And Ares supposed that was true. He had always been in *this* war. He had been dropped in it at birth.

But all that meant was that he knew how best to aim, then take fire, at the man who had taught him how to fight—never realizing, apparently, that in so doing he betrayed his own weaknesses.

"Did I not tell you the good news?" he asked his father mildly. Almost kindly. "Pia has made me the happiest man alive. She has agreed to be my wife. I know you—and the kingdom—will extend us your deepest congratulations."

And the first wedding gift he received was the splintering sound of his father's decanter against the castle wall. It was such a touch of nostalgia he very nearly came over all emotional as he took his leave.

And it was not until he was on his plane, heading back toward the Southern Palace, that it dawned on Ares that he would have to figure out how best to share these glad tidings with the woman he had yet to ask to be the wife he'd never wanted.

CHAPTER NINE

ONE THING PIA's childhood had taught her, like it or not, was that a person could get used to anything.

No matter how outrageous or absurd things seemed, and no matter how certain she was that they might, in fact, kill her—they never did.

She had gotten used to her parents' excesses. The further removed she got from the operatic marriage of Eddie Combe and Alexandrina San Giacomo, the more she started to think of them as eccentrics, somehow unable to behave in any way other than the way they had. In a decade or so, she was sure, she would find herself nostalgic for her parents, their tempestuous relationship, and all those endless, theatrical fights she'd found so difficult to live through while growing up with them.

So, too, was Pia becoming used to her life in her very own prison of a palace.

She felt like Rapunzel, locked away in her little tower, visited by nothing and no one—save the man who came to her, mostly at night, and made her head spin around and around without laying so much as a finger on her.

Pia spent her days writing columns about fussy manners as stand-ins for deeper emotions, reading revolt-ing things about herself in the tabloids—then vowing to stop reading revolting things about herself in the tabloids—and repeating the same thing over and over.

Her nights were punctuated by unpredictable glimpses of Ares.

Would he appear in the doorway as the shadows grew long, not there one moment and then a great, brooding presence in her peripheral vision the next? Would he ask her to join him for a drink with a guarded look in his green eyes and the suggestion of a banked fire in the way he held his big body? Would she agree, then sip at fizzy water as he swirled stronger spirits in a tumbler, the silence thick and layered between them? Or would they go a few rounds of conversation that al-ways seemed so…fraught?

Pia never knew. She only knew that she looked for-ward to Ares's appearances with an unseemly amount of anticipation. And missed him when his duties kept him away.

She could admit to herself, when she wasn't making arch remarks about her prison tower, that she had always been a person better suited to life outside the glare of media attention and tabloid speculation. That night in New York had been the one and only time she'd tried to…be someone else.

Maybe, she told herself dourly in a voice that sounded a bit too much like one of Alexandrina's mild rebukes, *the reason Ares cannot bear to spend more than a few moments in your company, and no matter that you are carrying his children, is because he sees only that ter-rible lie when he looks at you.*

She didn't like to think about that. But how could she not? Pia was not beautiful. She was nothing like her mother. A man like Ares could have anyone, and had. Why would he want to be tethered for the rest of his life to *her*?

Pia had thought she'd come to terms with her looks—or lack thereof—a long time ago. It was a natural consequence of being Alexandrina San Giacomo's only daughter. She had been destined to be a disappointment from the day she was born.

But she hadn't marinated on that sad fact in a long time. Apparently, being hugely pregnant and mostly alone, locked up in a castle like an embarrassment that needed to be hidden away from the light, got into a girl's head. And stayed there, hunkering down and breathing fire, whether she liked it or not.

"I will make sure that *our* branch of the family is better," she promised her babies every day, shifting around on her favorite chaise as the boys kicked at her. With more and more vigor as the days rolled by and they grew inside her. "I promise."

Pia was well into her seventh month of pregnancy when she discovered that her family had more branches than she knew.

Because it turned out that she and Matteo had another brother.

A half brother, Dominik, that their mother had given away when she was a teenager, long before she'd become an icon.

A scandalous little fact about her mother—her family—that Pia discovered by reading a tabloid.

"Did you know about this?" Pia asked Matteo in

disbelief, reaching him on some business trip some-where. When she knew he did, as the papers seemed to suggest that the new brother was dating Matteo's personal assistant—who had always returned Pia's calls before, yet was failing to do so at present. "How long have you known *we have another relative* and not told me?"

"It's not as if you've been available, Pia," Matteo said, and she would have said it was impossible for him to sound any colder than he already did. But he proved her wrong.

"I think by 'available' you mean, 'sitting in a room you might accidentally enter,'" Pia said, with a little more asperity than she normally showed her brother. Or anyone. "When the common definition also in-cludes this device I'm calling you on right now. It's very handy for the sharing of important news, like brand-new family members appearing full grown. Or even to say hello."

"If you wish to be kept up-to-date on everyday con-cerns, you would have to actually make that known," Matteo retorted. "Instead of running away from your own father's funeral and hiding out somewhere."

Pia had never thought of herself as a particular heir to the famous Combe temper. But she was so angry then, and possibly something else that she didn't know how to name, that the rest of the conversation stayed something of a blur to her.

And when she hung up, all she could think about was her mother.

Vain, beautiful, magnetic, impossible, deliriously compelling Alexandrina, who Pia had always wanted so desperately to please. And who Pia had always failed to please.

And who Pia had always thought had locked her away in that convent out of shame. Spite, perhaps. Or simple disinterest in a daughter who was so much less.

It had never occurred to her that when her mother told her that wrapping her up in cotton wool was a gift, Alexandrina had meant it. Just as it had never crossed Pia's mind that her mother's life could ever have been anything less than perfect. Or if not perfect, exactly as she'd wanted it.

Pia hardly knew how to think about a different Alexandrina. A woman who was…a person. A woman who had carried a child, just as Pia was doing now, and had given it away. An act of grace or shame, sorrow or hope, that Pia literally could not imagine living through herself.

Thinking of Alexandrina so young, and faced with such a tough decision…knocked Pia's world off balance. The Alexandrina she'd known was so smooth and polished. Even when she fought with Eddie. And had certainly not been harboring any deep hurts.

And maybe that was the hardest part of grief. It was always changing. Growing, expanding, shifting to fit whatever little pockets it found.

She had to assume it would always be that way.

And she was still sorting through what it meant to have a brother she didn't know—who, for all she knew, might want nothing to do with the family that had abandoned him long ago—when she looked up to find her very own Prince Not Quite Charming standing there in the doorway. The way he liked to do.

"How long have you been standing there?" she asked, her hands on her belly, still caught up in those confronting thoughts about her mother.

"What does it matter?" he asked, brooding and dark.

Pia forced a smile she didn't feel. "I've resigned myself to the cyber spying. It's your laptop and I have nothing to hide. Look through it at will if you feel you must. But I don't understand why it's necessary for you to lurk about your own palace like this."

"I do not lurk." His voice was even darker then, and there was a considering sort of gleam in his green gaze. "It is not my fault you are unobservant when it comes to your surroundings."

"Well, Ares—" she began, hotly.

But he held up a hand before she could continue down one of their familiar little paths that always led to the same place. Parry, retreat, regroup—and parry again. Back and forth they would go, until it was difficult to tell who struck whom. And who left the most marks.

"Come dine with me," he said, to her shock.

That did not usually happen. Ares was usually out for dinner, at this or that ball that Pia could follow on social media or in the papers the next day—not that she did such a thing. As that might be interpreted as too much interest in the man.

And maybe it was the novelty that had her biting her own tongue. She shifted, standing up—which took leveraging herself off the arm of the chaise these days—and then crossing to him.

He held out his hand as she approached. And Pia took it.

And it was as if the balance shifted. Or her world, still off its axis, tilted even more sharply. It felt as if the floors beneath her feet suddenly slanted terrifically, leaving her head spinning.

It wasn't just his touch. Or it wasn't only that. It was that solemn look, grave and intent, in those green eyes of his. Pia was sure she hadn't seen him look at her like that since...

But she didn't dare say it. She didn't dare think it.

And as Ares took her hand, then led her down the halls of the palace, she was buffeted by the memories of what happened between them that night in New York. When he had taken her hand like this and led her out of that party, and then all these restless things inside her had shifted into heat. Fire.

All that longing and need, greed and revelation.

It all kept washing over her, memory after memory.

He led her to the wing of the palace she knew was set aside for his exclusive use, and into a private dining room. It could have comfortably fit a crowd, but the table was set up to feel intimate, with a view over the ocean as the last of the sunset spread pink and orange over the horizon. Pia couldn't help thinking about the fact that they had skipped this part in New York. The sit down, have a meal, and learn about each other part.

This felt...remedial and precious, at once.

She found she was afraid to break the silence.

"I'm surprised you're here," she made herself say because it was best to rip the bandage off and dive straight in—another one of her father's favorite sayings. "Your social calendar is always so full."

"I canceled it."

"You mean, tonight's engagement?"

"All of it," Ares said.

And then did not expand on that statement at all.

The staff swept in, laying out the first course, but Pia hardly noticed it. And the babies must have sensed her agitation—or maybe it was anticipation, or something far more insidious, like longing—and as she rubbed her hand over her belly, she received a volley of kicks.

She must have sighed a little, because when she looked up, Ares was frowning at her. Not from down the length of a banquet table, but from much, much closer. Within reach.

"Is something happening?" he asked.

Aside from the hand he'd offered her tonight, Ares hadn't touched her since her first night here. And even then, it seemed to her that he had gone out of his way to avoid touching her belly. Yet when she looked at him now, he had the oddest expression on his face.

There was no doubt that he was focusing all his attention on her. On her belly, to be more precise, where her hand rubbed at the tiny little foot inside.

"One of them is kicking," she told him. "Which means the other one will likely join in any second now and make it a football match."

Ares looked as astonished as he did uncertain then. "Now? As you sit there?"

"Do you…? Do you want to feel it yourself?" Pia offered, surprised by the vulnerability she heard in her own voice.

And worse, the hope.

Ares rose from his chair, rounding the corner of the table that separated them. Then, without skipping a beat, he slid down before her. And there was a look on his face that she had never seen before. His green eyes were dark.

Pia smiled. "Give me your hands."

She didn't wait for him to offer them. She reached over, took his hands in hers, and brought them firmly against her belly.

And, sure enough, the moment his hands slid into place over her bump, two different sets of feet reacted.

Pia watched Ares's face. The jolt of surprise. The understanding of what he was feeling beneath his palms.

And then, like a dose of pure sunshine, the wonder.

"Does it hurt?" he asked, his voice hushed.

"Sometimes it's uncomfortable," she said softly. "Or surprising. Or if one of them stretches out and presses their feet up against my ribs, that aches."

He shifted, coming down on his knees before her chair, and his hands were suddenly everywhere. Moving all over her bump, as if testing it. Learning its shape.

And the more he ran his hands over her, the more Pia liked it. And in a way that had nothing at all to do with their babies or any kicking. She felt the shift in her like a flame leaping into life, from coals she'd imagined were cold.

It turned out they were only smoldering.

When Ares looked up at her again, there was a gleaming heat in his gaze that she recognized. Oh, how she recognized it. How she *felt* it.

"Pia," he said, his voice low. Hot.

And an unmistakable invitation.

Pia couldn't take this. Not for another moment. Ares

was so close, his hands on her, that look of marvel and need on his beautiful face.

How could she do anything but melt? And as she melted and ran hot, that liquid greed bloomed inside her, low in her belly and deep between her legs.

Where only Ares had ever touched her.

His gaze searched hers.

Did she whisper his name? Or did it live in her already? Always?

Whichever it was, it made Pia lose her head completely. She leaned forward, slid her hands to hold his face, and then settled her mouth to his as if she might die then and there if she couldn't taste him again.

She felt him groan, low and deep, as if it came from the depths of him. She felt his big, athletic body shake slightly, as if from the force of the same wild sensation that swept through her, too.

And then his mouth opened beneath hers and he took control.

And when he kissed her, Pia forgot that she wasn't beautiful.

When Ares kissed her, Pia felt as if she was made entirely of glory. Light and lovely, sweet and right, strung out on the heaven in his every touch. All that hot perfection.

Ares moved closer, one hand curling around her neck as if to guide her where he wanted her. The other stayed put on her belly.

She felt untethered by her own need, and anchored at the same time.

He made her feel like she could fly. Like this was flying.

Ares kissed her and he kissed her, and Pia didn't know which one of them was trying harder to move closer. To take the kiss deeper. She was frustrated that he wasn't closer. She wanted his skin on hers, his hands on her bare flesh.

She *wanted*.

Ares groaned again, then shifted back. His mouth curved at the sound of protest she made, and he pulled her up from her chair. He set her briefly on her feet, but only briefly, because he moved then to lift her into his arms.

And here she was absurdly pregnant, yet he was still making her feel as if she weighed nothing at all.

"Ares, you can't—"

"So help me God, Pia," Ares growled down at her. "If you're about to tell me that I cannot lift you when I have very clearly already done so, I will be tempted to drop you over the side of the balcony."

And she didn't think he was likely to do that.

But she didn't finish her sentence, either.

He bore her outside, onto the balcony he had just mentioned, wide and open. He lay her down on a wide, low chaise, and followed her. Then stretched out beside her so they were finally—*finally*—touching, head to toe.

And that was almost too much.

But Ares took her mouth again, and they both groaned at the heat. The mad, glorious kick of hunger.

He kissed her and he kissed her, and she kissed him back with all the longing and need she'd kept inside her all this time. All that delirious fire that he stoked in her.

Only him.

Ares was dressed for one of his royal engagements, but he pulled back to shrug out of his jacket and his shirt, giving Pia access to those wide shoulders of his and better yet, his mouthwatering chest.

She took instant advantage, moving her hands over him and letting herself exult in his strength. His heat.

Each and every perfect ridge and tempting hollow.

And everything was too hot. Too good.

He found her breasts, so plump and big now. And he made such a deep, male sound of approval as he filled his hands with them that Pia forgot to be self-conscious. He pushed up the loose blouse she wore and freed her breasts from the front clasp of her bra.

Then he bent his head to take a nipple into his mouth.

And the sensation was so intense, so wild and over-whelming. It shot through her, a molten hot line from her nipple to her hungry sex, that Pia felt herself pull too tight—

Then she simply shattered, there and then.

Ares let out a laugh of dark delight that shivered its way through Pia like a new, bright flame. Then he moved to her other nipple, taking it into his mouth in the same greedy, demanding way. She tried to breathe. She tried to fight it off, but he only sucked a little harder—

And that was it. She went tumbling from one peak to the next, and broke apart all over again.

"I can't believe how sensitive you are now," he murmured, his mouth on her belly. "Let's test it, shall we?"

Then—slowly, carefully, ruthlessly—he stripped her of the loose, easy clothes she wore.

And Pia was too busy falling to pieces, and gasping

for breath, and crying out his name, to think about the things that would have torn her apart at any other time. Her size, for example. How fat she must look. How different than before.

But she was too busy losing herself in Ares's mouth. Beneath his clever, wicked hands.

She didn't notice when he stripped out of the rest of his clothes, too, because his hands found their way between her legs, teasing her slick flesh until she broke apart again.

And again.

And then, finally, Ares went and knelt before the chaise, pulling her to the edge and opening her legs wide. He held himself there, moving between her thighs. Only then did he find her soft, wet heat with the hardest part of him.

His gaze lifted to hers. Pia held her breath. And Ares pushed his way inside.

Slowly. Carefully.

Almost as if this was sacred. Beautiful.

As if she was.

"Pia," he murmured, as if her name was a prayer.

And then he set about his devotions, one perfect thrust after the next.

And she was already coming apart. She was already in pieces. Over and over again, as if the pleasure was a wave and she was caught in the undertow, tossed and tumbling and wild with it.

She lost count of how many times he brought her to that glorious cliff and tossed her over, only to catch her on the way down and do it all again.

It was too much, and it was beautiful and perfect,

and Pia never wanted to go without it—without him, without *this*—again.

She heard a distant sound and realized that she was saying those things out loud, but she didn't have it in her to mind that, either. Not when she was captured in that undertow, lost in the whirl of it.

Pia shook and she shook, she came down a little only to feel him surge deep inside her again, and she shook even more.

Until she thought she might become the shaking.

And finally, when he hit his own cliff, Ares gathered her to him. He dropped his head into the crook of her neck and called out her name as he shattered at last.

And she understood, now, Pia thought in a kind of wonder when she surfaced to find herself tucked up on that chaise, Ares having crawled up next to her like a kind of warm, gloriously male blanket.

It had been so hard, after New York, to understand why she'd behaved the way she had there. Why she'd done those things, and so easily and carelessly when that wasn't her. That wasn't how she behaved.

But she got it now. It was this. It was Ares.

It was extraordinary.

He was remarkable.

And it was no wonder that she had never been the same since.

She found herself running her fingers up and down her belly, in the absent way she often did, and she smiled when Ares did it, too, from beside her. Tracing patterns this way and that.

Introducing himself, she thought when one baby kicked.

Letting them know who he was, she thought when the other followed suit.

"Pia," Ares said, in that low, marvelous voice of his that she loved to feel roll over her like the sweet, thick breeze from the sea before them. "You are the mother of my sons."

"That's me," she said softly, and her smile trembled a bit on her mouth. "Like it or not."

He looked up from her belly, leveling all that green intensity on her. His expression was grave. "I want you to marry me."

It was an order. A royal command.

And what surprised Pia was how deeply, how passionately she wanted to obey him.

But what did she know about marriage? Nothing but what she'd seen growing up. And certainly nothing that let her imagine two people so unevenly matched could make it work. She'd watched her parents' marriage explode time and time again, sometimes in the same evening. She'd watched it fall apart a thousand times, though they'd stayed together. She'd watched the games they played with and at each other, and the pieces they'd carved from each other that she didn't think they'd ever gotten back.

And Eddie and Alexandrina had been a love story for the ages.

Pia didn't see any reason why she should subject her babies to a far grimmer, far less exalted version of her parents' marriage. All the struggle and pain and yet none of the love.

How could she subject herself to that? And worse

still, how could she make her babies grow up like that?
Hadn't it been hard enough for her?

She lay there on the balcony with the sea as their wit-
ness, naked and replete, still spinning in all that sensation and sweet hunger. She reached over and slid her
hand over Ares's, holding him to her.

And she said no.

"No." She said it distinctly. "I won't marry you. But
you are the father to my sons, Ares. That won't change.
We don't have to be married. We can just…be parents."

He was quiet for a long, taut moment.

"And how do you think that will work when I take
the throne?" he asked mildly, though Pia wasn't fooled
by his almost offhand tone. "Will the two princes have
alternate weekends with their father, the King of Atilia,
and then spend the rest of the time in some godforsaken
Yorkshire village?"

"We'll figure it out, one way or another." Pia made
herself smile at him, though it felt like a risk when his
green eyes were so dark. "With or without my beloved,
godforsaken Yorkshire."

Ares rolled to his feet. Then he reached down and
pulled her up from the chaise, letting her stand there
before him as the night air danced over them.

And as Pia longed for more.

"I mean to have you as my wife," he told her, starkly.

"No," she said again, and felt something hitch in her
as she said it, as if the longing was tangled up on itself.
"No, you don't. You want to marry me for the babies,
but it has nothing to do with *me*. You don't want *me* for
a wife. You want your babies' mother."

"Why can't I want both?"

"No," she said again. Calmly and firmly, despite that tumult inside her that she feared was something even more embarrassing.

Like stark, desperate yearning, despite everything.

And Pia expected him to argue. To rage, perhaps, the way her father would have. Or go dark and broody, the way she'd seen him do before.

But Ares only smiled.

CHAPTER TEN

PIA DIDN'T KNOW what she'd expected. Perhaps she thought that having been rejected, Ares would go off somewhere. Lick his wounds with his favorite whiskey. Pretend the conversation had never happened.

Instead, he helped her dress, pulling the softly elegant knits into place. Then he ushered her back into the dining room and took his time helping her into her seat. He sat—too close to her—at the entirely too intimate table, and they…had a perfectly civilized dinner.

Complete with finger bowls at the end.

"And if I drink mine?" she dared ask him. "Will you do the appropriate thing as host? All to make me feel comfortable?"

But this was why Pia wrote columns about seemingly insignificant things like whether or not to send thank-you notes—yes, always—and whether one should flout convention in matters such as the wearing of white in the off-season—of course, if you can pull it off.

Because it was never about the finger bowls. It was about taking care of other people.

It was about whether or not she felt safe with him when Pia didn't know if she'd ever been safe in her life.

Or how she could possibly know the difference when she didn't know what such a thing felt like.

"Marry me," Ares replied, his green gaze tight on hers. Because he was relentless and he clearly didn't mind her knowing it. "And you will see exactly what kind of host I am."

Pia did not drink from her finger bowl. And she was shaken all over again, if in a markedly different fashion, by the fact Ares hadn't let it go. If he was chastened or upset by her refusal, he didn't seem to show it.

After dinner, he escorted her out into the hallway, but when she turned to make her way back toward her wing of the palace, he held fast to her arm.

"I think not," he said quietly. "We have only just begun to take the edge off, have we not?"

"The edge?" Pia repeated because she didn't dare imagine that he meant what she thought he did. What her body certainly hoped he did, as it shivered everywhere, inside and out, when she was sure she shouldn't have been able to feel a thing. Not when she'd felt too much already.

"*Cara mia*, it has been much too long since New York. My hunger for you has yet to be quenched."

Maybe she should have argued. Held fast to some or other standard…but Pia wanted him more than she wanted to fight him.

All she did was nod. Once.

Ares did not do a good job of hiding his sharp, hot grin then. He led her to his vast suite of rooms, instead. And he laid her out on his massive bed, clearly made for kings, and crawled up over her to learn every inch of her body all over again.

And when she was writhing, and out of her head once more, he turned her over. He settled her on her hands and knees, so he could slide into her from behind.

That time, she screamed his name when she burst apart.

Every time she burst apart.

And that was only the beginning of his campaign.

He had all her things moved into his rooms and when she objected, merely lifted an arrogant brow.

"I do not wish to traipse down a mile of palace corridors when I could more easily turn over and find you in my bed, Pia," he told her. Loftily.

And maybe Pia was weak. But she liked sleeping in his bed. And she liked it even more when he turned over and woke her up.

He still maintained his schedule of events. Royal necessities that meant he was always trotting off to this or that.

But he came home more than he had before.

And Pia laughed at herself when she realized that was the word she used now. *Home.* To describe this mad, fairy-tale palace where she was locked away from the world.

Or maybe, something inside her suggested, *this is where you get to retreat from the world.*

When had her prison begun to feel like a *retreat*?

She found she stopped looking at the tabloids, particularly as they now starred both of her brothers and their various romantic entanglements. It wasn't only that she didn't want the nasty, gossipy version of her family in her head. It was more that she liked focusing on her own life.

Because she had a life, for once. She was growing brand-new humans inside her. She was carrying on with her writing. And she had Ares, after a fashion.

He taught her things it was impossible to learn in a single night.

And if her giant, pregnant body was any kind of hindrance, he never showed it. He seemed perfectly capable of coming up with new, improved ways to make sure they were both comfortable while they explored each other.

Sometimes he talked. He made dark, delicious promises, then followed through on each and every one of them.

Other times, he was dark, silent, and impossibly beautiful as he moved over her, in her.

One afternoon, after he had made her sob, scream, and then beg a bit for good measure, Ares sprawled beside her. The bed was big, wide, and rumpled beneath them. Up above, the ceiling fan turned lazily, keeping the air moving. Pia could hear the ever-present sound of the ocean outside, crashing over the rocks and surging against the shore.

And Ares was hot and beautiful, all leashed power and male grace as he lay there beside her, his fingers laced with hers.

No matter what happened, Pia knew she would always remember this moment. When she'd almost forgot her body entirely, or could only seem to remember what he could do to it.

Beautiful, something in her whispered. *He makes you feel beautiful.*

"Marry me," he said, the way he always did. He had

asked her to marry him so many times now that she thought it had lost its power. Almost. Now it was just a thing he said.

Pass the salt, please. Marry me.

Pia laughed. "You know I can't."

"I know no such thing."

She sighed, shifting in an attempt to get comfortable. "You were very clear that you wanted no wife. No children. And the children were a surprise to us both, but I think we will do very well now that we've adjusted to it all. But why add marriage to the mix?"

"I remember seeing your parents at a ball," Ares said into the quiet of the room, with only the ocean outside as accompaniment. "It was perhaps ten years ago now. It was a ghastly sort of state affair, bristling with diplomats and career socialites."

As he always did, now, Ares moved his hand over her belly. Finding one baby's head, and the other's pair of feet. Saying hello to his sons. Pia had grown used to the patterns he drew there. The way she sometimes drifted off to sleep and woke to find Ares crooning nonsense to her belly.

She hardly dared admit how that made her feel. Riddled with hope. Laced through with sweetness. So full of impossible, unwieldy emotion, she felt it was one more part of her set to burst. At any moment.

"I never knew my parents to subject themselves to anything grim or ghastly," Pia said, trying to rally when everything felt too emotional these days. She was in her eighth month, and twins were usually early. Her time with them as part of her was almost over. And so, too, was her time with Ares nearing its natural conclusion.

She could feel it with every breath. "They much preferred to be the life of the liveliest parties they could find."

"I imagine it was a business affair for your father," Ares said. "There were stultifying speeches, as there always are. Much self-congratulation. Then the dancing began. There were the usual awkward couplings of diplomats, their wives, and so on. These things are typically excruciating. But then your parents took the floor."

Pia thought she knew where this was going. She smiled, settling more fully on her side. "My parents loved to dance."

"That was instantly apparent. I don't know anything about their marriage, or not anything that wasn't twisted to sell papers, but I did see them dance. I saw the way they looked at each other."

"Not only as if there was no one else in the room," Pia said softly, remembering. "But as if no one else existed at all."

"My own parents did not dance unless it was strictly necessary for reasons of highest protocol," Ares told her, propping himself up on one elbow and regarding her, an odd sort of gleam in his green eyes that made them seem burnished with gold. "And when they did, they did their best never to gaze at each other at all. I watched them dance at the same ball ten years ago and I imagine it was perfectly clear to everyone in the room how little esteem they held for each other."

"Did they not...?" Pia didn't quite know how to phrase the question.

Ares let out a laugh, but it was tinged with bitterness. "My father liked to indulge his temper. When it was aimed at me, he liked to throw things against walls. I am only grateful that he contained that rage to me alone and never aimed it at my mother." He shook his head. "They say he is a decent enough ruler, but he was a cold, unfeeling husband and is a terrible father."

"You don't have to talk about this," Pia said quietly, when she thought he wouldn't go on.

Ares's eyes glittered. "My mother provided him with the requisite heir, thus securing the bloodline and the kingdom, which was all he cared about. Once that was accomplished, he felt perfectly justified in pursuing his extracurricular interests. Without caring overmuch if that might hurt her feelings. In fact, I think I can say with perfect honesty that I have never known my father to care about anyone's feelings. Ever."

Pia tried to pull up pictures of the king of Atilia and his late queen in her head. And more, tried to think of them as people instead of pictures anyone could look at.

"Your father cheated on your mother?" she asked.

"Constantly." Ares smiled, but it was little more than the sharp edge of his teeth. "And enthusiastically. Quantity over quality, if my sources are correct."

Pia let out a breath, and directed her attention to the place where their hands were still linked.

"I think my parents cheated on each other as well," she told him, though she'd never admitted that out loud before. No matter what the papers said. "I know they loved each other, madly and wildly. Everyone knows that. But part of that kind of love is all about hurting each other. I think the glory was in the coming back together, so they always seemed to look for new ways to break apart."

Ares lifted her hand and brought it to his mouth. He pressed his lips against her knuckles and Pia's heart instantly careened around inside of her chest. Fizzy and mad, as if they weren't already naked. As if they hadn't already spent hours making each other moan.

His gaze was intent on hers. "I never wanted to marry because I watched a royal Atilian marriage play out right in front of me. My father was a brute, always. And my mother was always so sad. I never wanted that for any woman bound to me, whether by duty or desire."

He reached over and brushed her hair back from her face, and Pia didn't want to see the look on his then. It was…too open. Too complicated.

It made her heart pick up its pace.

"But I am willing to take the chance that you and I can make something different, between us. Something better, Pia."

She shook her head at him, afraid that if she investigated any further she would discover that the lump in her throat and the glassiness in her eyes could tip over too quickly into tears. And would.

Because she kept telling herself that he was joking. Or if not *joking*, precisely, saying these things she'd always wanted to hear because he thought he could convince her that way. Not because he actually believed them.

But the trouble was, she *wanted* to believe him. And the more of these sorts of things he said, the more she wanted to believe.

When she knew better.

"Ares," she began.

"We are magic in bed, Pia," he said, in a voice as

intense as the way he looked at her. "That is how we came to be here in the first place. Is the worst thing in the world to think we might as well make it official?"

"You're the one who gave me a lesson in the lines of Atilian succession." She wanted to roll out of the bed and storm away. But it took her too long to do such things—or anything—these days. So she settled for rolling away from him, and pushing herself up into sitting position.

And as she did, she was suddenly too aware of how naked she was. How huge her breasts had become. How misshapen her belly was, sticking so far out, with her belly button protruding.

"Yes," Ares was saying, watching her. "I'm concerned about the lines of succession. Should I not be? I told you the day of your father's funeral that it was no small thing to claim you carry my child. That hasn't changed. If anything, the closer we get to your due date, the more serious the matter becomes."

"Because all of a sudden now you care deeply about these things?"

"I may not have set out to make myself heirs." And there was something granite in his voice. In the gaze he leveled on her. It made something deep inside her start to tremble. "But they exist. They will be here sooner rather than later. And I would prefer it if they had access to all the rights and privileges their position as my heirs allows them."

"Why?" She was rubbing her belly, and made herself stop. "You felt one way about all of this, then you interacted with your father and everything changed. It's hard not to think you simply want to defy him."

His expression changed, and she wondered if he'd thought she didn't know. That she hadn't seen the pictures of the two of them—*King Damascus Takes Errant Heir to Task!* the papers had cackled—and seen the dark look on Ares's face.

"What do you think will happen?" he asked her, and she thought she hated it most when he sounded so *patient*. So *reasonable*.

"Do you need me to explain to you where babies come from, Ares?" she asked him, proud that she kept her voice calm.

"The world already believes you are pregnant with at least one of my children," he replied, only that cool gleam in his eyes indicating that he was even aware of the question she'd asked. "Let us say, for the sake of argument, that I let you go right now. And you set out into the world, footloose and fancy-free as you claim to want. You're lucky enough not to be impoverished, which means you will no doubt be capable of raising these babies just fine on your own."

"I've been making this argument for months."

"But the world will continue to think they are mine, no matter what lies we tell or lengths we take to conceal that truth. And what then?"

"What do you mean, 'what then?' Rumors are just rumors—"

"Rumors are rumors, yes. But thrones are thrones, *cara mia*." And she didn't know what that note in his voice was then. Or that look in his eyes. Only that it made her tremble—again. "And we may have grown progressive in these latter days. We prefer to have our fights in ballot boxes rather than in the streets or on poppy fields. But that does not change the fact that you will be raising two boys with a direct claim to the throne of Atilia. I understand that means nothing to you, but I assure you—it will not only mean something to my people, it will mean even more to whoever succeeds me."

"Succeeds you?" She didn't understand.

"I will take the throne, and then I will die," Ares said, with certain matter-of-factness that made her want to scream. Or do *something* to protest the ruthless inevitability in his voice. "And whoever comes next, whether it be a cousin or whatever issue my father manages to rustle up in his waning years, your boys will be out there. Some will inevitably claim that one of them is the rightful king. And do you know what will happen then?"

"Let me guess," Pia said, more sharply than she intended, surely. But she couldn't seem to pull herself back. "Another war."

"The blood of Atilia runs in my veins," Ares told her, his voice low and insistent. "It is poison. It is war and it is pain. And I am sorry to be the bearer of this news, but it is in you, too, now. It is in those boys. It is who we are."

"I don't know what any of that means." But she had moved herself back as she spoke, so she was sitting up against the headboard. And she was watching him as if he might snap at any moment, and then God only knew what might happen. Or what she might do. "Of course there's nothing in your blood. Royalty is not a virus."

"I beg to differ," Ares said, with a short sort of laugh, bitter and dark. "Royalty is power, nothing more and nothing less. And power infects. It could be that some successor seeks you out, and tries to neutralize any threat that your boys present. That is horrifying enough to contemplate."

That he had already contemplated that stung Pia. When she hadn't. She hadn't thought much beyond her pregnancy. She had been too busy settling here in this palace of his. She had been too focused on her hopeless little heart.

She was already a bad mother and her children weren't born yet.

"But there is also another possibility," Ares said in that same powerfully mild way that was wreaking havoc on her. "Who knows who our sons will grow up to become? Either one of them might decide that they deserve their birthright. What do you plan to do then?"

Pia's heart clattered around in her chest. And all she could seem to do was beat herself up for the possibilities she hadn't considered.

She tried to shake it off—because she could beat herself up on her own time. She didn't have to do it when Ares was watching her like this, close and very nearly *ferocious*. "So your position is that we should marry, and that will somehow…prevent your sons from taking the throne? Or prevent someone else from taking it? Or prevent…something else? I'm not following you."

"Pia—"

"And I've already told you that I won't restrict your access from them. I mean that. But a marriage between you and me isn't about them. It's about me."

She hated the fact that her voice cracked on that last word. That it gave her away so completely. That it showed him things she didn't want him to know.

"Pia," he said again, even more calmly than before.

And this time, she didn't care how hard it was. She got herself to the edge of the bed, and shoved herself off. She had to stand still for a moment, her hand on the small of her back, and she almost burst into tears because she wanted to storm away. But there was no *storming* in her current state. There was only waddling. And she already felt bad enough. She certainly didn't need to *waddle* in front of him. Naked.

She grabbed at the coverlet that had been kicked to the foot of the bed. It was something spun from gold and unicorn dust, or so it appeared, like everything else in this place. Pia wrapped it around herself like a makeshift dress.

And she didn't understand how she had let all this happen.

It was as if she hadn't quite been paying attention. There had been all that mind-altering sex to distract her. And the exquisite sweetness of their nights together made her forget herself during the day. He'd moved her into his rooms and she'd just…let it happen. She hadn't put up so much as a token protest. In fact, it hadn't occurred to her to protest.

She'd been enjoying herself too much.

And now she was in her eighth month of this pregnancy. She was enormous. And she couldn't tell if she was finding it hard to breathe because she was emotional, or because she had two babies pressed up hard against…everything.

But she knew that she'd miscalculated. Greatly. She had more than miscalculated.

Because what she couldn't tell him was that while he

had been indulging himself, and playing whatever game this was with her, she had been doing something far more dangerous. He had been playing a long game, trying to get her to marry him for his own suspect reasons.

But Pia had been falling in love.

And she had to bite back a little sob as that word poured through her, so bright and hot she was shocked he couldn't *see* it.

She couldn't think of anything more stupid. Or embarrassing. But it was true. She had fallen in love with Ares. If she was honest, she suspected that it had happened at first sight at that party in New York. Because she had never been affected by any other man.

But one look at Ares and she'd wandered off with him, happily. Then she'd gotten herself wildly, irrevocably knocked up. And to add insult to injury, as was apparently her specialty, she'd gone off with him again at her own father's funeral.

She'd let him lock her up here. And sure, she had a thousand excuses for herself. There were guards. There was only one road out and it was closely watched. But the truth was, she hadn't tried very hard to get away from him after that first night.

Pia had told herself she was nesting. That was what pregnant women did—every article she found online said so. She wrote columns about trusting one's gut and how best to handle awkward social interactions, while all the while she was handling her relationship with this man just about as badly as it was possible to do.

Because Ares might have decided he wanted something other than what he'd told her he wanted at the start, but it didn't matter. Because any way she looked at it, what he really wanted was his sons without the trouble of custody agreements. Which was fair enough.

But it felt even more brutal now that he didn't want *her*.

He would have sex with her. Extremely good sex, if what he said was true about this wild, greedy thing they shared. But he didn't love her. He couldn't love her. He hadn't been looking for *her* when he'd found her at Combe Manor that day. He'd been on one of his royal engagements, doing his duty to the family.

When Pia knew, thanks to her father, that when a man loved a woman he could not rest. He would seek her out, no matter what damage it did. *No matter what.*

It was long past time Pia faced the facts here, no matter how little she liked them.

"I don't understand why everything changed," she said to him, trying to keep her panic tamped down. And worse, that bright beacon of a word she couldn't say and a thing she shouldn't feel. "You were very certain about the things you didn't want."

"It's not a question about what I want," Ares said, his green gaze hooded. "It's a question of what is right."

He was still on the bed, lounging there in that seemingly careless way of his. And it made her heart kick at her. *He* did, even now.

She tightened her grip on the coverlet. "Because somehow, what is right involves war in the blood and something about poison. Oh, yes, and infectious power."

"I want to make you my queen," Ares said, and he no longer sounded quite so mild. "Do you not understand that part of it?"

"I understand it," Pia heard herself say, though she hardly recognized her own voice. "That's the problem."

She turned her head away, not sure what might be written all over her face then. What he might see. She wrapped the coverlet even tighter around her, bitterly aware that the only thing she could wrap around herself at all these days was a piece of fabric that had been made to stretch across a bed. A very large bed.

Her throat ached, but she made herself speak anyway. "I'm the size of the barn. But even if I were not, you and I both know what I look like on any normal day."

There was only silence, and Pia was forced to turn back and look at him.

Ares only gazed back at her, a baffled sort of look on his gorgeous face.

Pia made a frustrated sound. "I'm not a queen!"

"You are a queen if you marry a king. It is really that simple."

"The very idea is laughable, Ares. Do you understand me?" Her voice sounded like a sob. But she couldn't seem to stop herself. She couldn't do a single thing to avert this horror as it happened. "People would *laugh*."

CHAPTER ELEVEN

For a moment there was nothing but the echo of Pia's raw words hanging there between them.

She wanted to snatch them back with her own two hands. Her fingers twitched as if they might try, all on their own.

"Now I am the one not following you." Ares looked bemused and haughty at once, every inch of him royal as he lay there on the bed as if he was entirely at his ease. Perhaps he was. "People would laugh why, exactly?"

Pia was shaking. Everywhere. She wrapped her hand around the nearest bedpost, hoping it would steady her. Hoping something would, when the floor seemed so treacherous beneath her. She couldn't believe he was going to make her say it out loud. And worse, she couldn't tell if he was taunting her.

"A man like you is on a certain level," she said, pulling herself up as straight as she could, despite the weight of her belly. And the far greater weight of her shame. "You must be aware of this."

"You mean that I am the Crown Prince? Yes, Pia. I am aware of it. It is the sort of thing they tend to tell you from a very young age."

"I don't mean the fact that you're a prince, although that's part of it. I mean… You." She waved her hand in his direction. Trying to take in all of it, all of *him*, as he lounged there. Golden, rangy and athletic, as if someone had come in and carved a god from marble and breathed life into the stone. "You are a beautiful man. You are meant to find a beautiful wife. No one would accept a queen like me for a man like you."

Ares stared at her for a long while. As the panic and worry inside her intensified, she focused on strange things. Like the muscle in his jaw that clenched, seemingly of its own volition. Or the way his green eyes seemed darker. More dangerous.

"I will take it that what you are telling me is that you do not believe you are beautiful," he said. Eventually.

Pia made herself smile, though she was terribly afraid that the humiliation of this might take her out at the knees. Or maybe she only hoped it would.

"My mother was widely held to be the most beautiful woman in the world. Yes, she had her issues. She was not always kind, or good. Or even polite. And judging by the pills and the alcohol she took at the end, she was also not very happy." She blew out a breath, and hoped he couldn't hear how it shook. "My brother thinks it was deliberate, but I don't. For a while I thought maybe I pushed her to it, and my father, too, having fallen pregnant the way I did. But now I think it was an accident, because the one thing I know about Alexandrina San Giacomo is that she had no intention of going out with a whimper."

Alexandrina had been an opera heroine, always. Any death scene she'd planned would have been long-winded, theatrical, and would have required a vast audience. Most important, she would have needed to make certain she stayed beautiful throughout.

Pia didn't know when her certainty that she was to blame had…shifted. She suspected it had to do with spending all this time with Ares. All she knew for certain was that somehow, it had been a long while since she'd felt personal guilt about her parents' deaths. One had been an accident. The other had been inevitable. Her pregnancy had nothing to do with either.

Which didn't make it any easier.

She remembered that Ares was watching her. Waiting, all that leashed power of his coiled and tight.

"What my mother always had, what everyone knew and agreed on, was that she was beautiful. No matter how drunk, or tired, or under the weather. Men would stop in the street to stare. Sometimes they burst into song. Does that sound ridiculous?" She shrugged. "A serenade in the street was merely an unremarkable day in my mother's life. I grew up knowing exactly what *beautiful* meant. And seeing exactly what it looked like."

"I see." Ares's voice sounded almost…strangled.

"Do you?" she demanded.

Pia didn't understand what was sloshing around inside of her then. It was too much sensation. It was too much emotion. It was *too much*.

And maybe Alexandrina had it right. Maybe it was better to make everything an opera. Because at least then you could be in control of when the curtain went up, when it went down, and everything in between. How funny that she'd never understood that until now.

She took the coverlet from around her, and tossed it aside, the way her mother would have. With flourish.

"Do you really see?" she demanded. "Look at this body, Ares. It was never much to begin with, and after this? It will be a different body altogether. Forever. It will never snap back. There will be stretch marks, everywhere. And that's the least of it. I've seen pictures of my mother when she was pregnant. She looked like at any moment, someone might happen by and write a sonnet to her beauty."

"Is this an argument you truly wish to win?" he asked.

"It's not an argument. It's reality. I'm not my mother, and I'm certainly not beautiful like she was."

"I don't know how to say this," Ares said, as if he was choosing his words carefully. "But I cannot think of much I care less about than your mother's supposed beauty."

"It wasn't 'supposed.' It wasn't an opinion, it was a fact."

"Your mother was a lovely woman," Ares agreed, shrugging one shoulder. "But what of it? The world is filled with beautiful women."

"You're making my point for me," Pia said, wishing she hadn't tossed the coverlet aside. She could hardly go scrabbling after it now she'd made such a show of casting it off. She was forced to stand there instead, tall and proud, when she wanted nothing more than to curl up in a ball and cringe away into oblivion somewhere. "The world is filled with beautiful women, and you ought to go out and find yourself one of them."

"Pia. *Cara mia.*" And Ares looked as if he was biting back a smile, which Pia couldn't understand at all.

"Perhaps you do not understand to whom you are speaking. I am Crown Prince Ares of Atilia. I have dukedoms and earldoms to spare. I am, by definition and royal decree, possessed of the finest taste. Any woman who graces my arm is beautiful by virtue of her presence there. Obviously."

Pia opened her mouth to argue, but stopped when he rolled himself up to sitting position, never shifting his gaze from her face.

"But you? The mother of my children? The only woman alive I have ever asked to be my queen? *Of course* you are beautiful." He shrugged again, so arrogant and assured that it should have hurt him. Yet clearly did not. "It never occurred to me that you could imagine otherwise."

"You can't throw compliments at me and think that it will change the fact that I am not, in any way, the kind of woman a man like you goes for."

"I suggest you look down at your very pregnant belly," Ares said, his voice slightly less patient and mild. "I have already gone for you. Repeatedly."

"Stop saying these things!" She threw the words at him, unable to control her voice—or anything else—any longer. "I know what I look like. I know what I am. Pretending that I'm something else isn't going to get me to marry you."

"Then what will?"

And Pia kept trying to suck in more air. She couldn't seem to form another word.

And that was when Ares moved again. He rolled to his feet, then came to her, wrapping his hands around her shoulders and holding her up.

"You are the only woman I have ever asked to marry me," he told her, his voice serious and his gaze darkly intense. "But if that is not enough for you, think back to the party where we met. Why do you think I was drawn to you? At first, before we spoke a word to each other? If you are so misshapen, such a hideous troll—do you imagine it was curiosity that drew me to your side?"

This was ridiculous. Tears were spilling over, tracking their way down her cheeks, and Pia wanted to die. She wanted to sink to the floor of the palace, and be swept out to sea.

"I don't know," she said, her voice cracked and much too thick. "I looked up and you were…there."

"I was there because I saw you smile," Ares said. "I heard you laugh. I was there because I followed that smile across the room, simply because I wanted to get close to it. And then, when we met, I wanted to get even closer. None of that has changed."

"Ares…"

"Marry me because every time I have asked you to follow me so far, you have," he said, words in his eyes that she was afraid to believe in. "Follow me because I have yet to lead you anywhere you didn't like. You call this palace a prison, yet here we are, together—and it feels more to me like an escape. Marry me, Pia, and we will make our marriage another kind of refuge. The sort we can take with us wherever we go."

"You only want—"

"Our sons," he finished for her. "Yes, of course I want them. Let's raise them together."

And maybe she had always been this weak. Maybe

it was the way he made her feel, and she couldn't help herself. She liked it too much.

She knew better, but Ares looked at her as if she was beautiful. And when he did, she was tempted to believe it. Here, now, she did believe it.

And that belief trickled down into her, making her feel warm. Safe.

And there were worse things, surely. There were men who didn't want their own babies and who went to great lengths to avoid their responsibilities. There were men who didn't make her heart kick at her the way it did whenever Ares was near.

A whole world full of them, in fact.

There were marriages, especially amongst the sort of people she knew, that were little more than business transactions. There were cold, brittle unions, husbands and wives who were faithless, others who exulted in causing each other pain.

There were a thousand ways to have a terrible marriage.

But maybe what that meant was that Pia could decide how to make hers a good one. Or a decent one, anyway. Better than most. And maybe there wasn't only one fairy-tale way to get there.

Maybe there were twin boys. A palace fit for Rapunzel. And months spent doing nothing but circling around and around the inevitable. Maybe there were wild, hot nights of sex and longing with the only man she'd ever wanted to touch.

Already that sounded better than half the marriages she'd ever heard of.

And Pia loved him, though she knew better than

that, too. She loved him even though she was sure that the years would pass and whatever protestations he'd made here tonight about her supposed beauty would fade. He would regret this. He might take his own father's path.

Pia knew that she would still love him then. That she would always love him. So what would be worse? Never having any part of this? Or losing what little she had?

In front of her, Ares shifted. He dropped onto his knees, his gaze locked to hers as the afternoon sun poured in and highlighted every last perfect, glorious inch of him.

Both of them were naked. Pia's belly was so big it could take over the whole of the room on its own, and maybe the world. Ares didn't put his hands there. Instead, he reached up and took hers in his.

"Pia," he said, very gravely. "Marry me. Be my queen and mother to my sons. And promise me that from time to time, you will smile at me the way you did in a stranger's party in Manhattan."

And her heart kicked at her, but she couldn't tell if it was signaling danger or excitement. Hope or anxiety. All of the above.

And she knew better. *She knew better.*

The worst thing she could possibly do was believe.

But her hands were in his much bigger ones. And his gaze was so serious that it made her flush a little.

And she had two baby boys inside her who deserved their father.

What do you deserve, dear girl? that voice inside asked her, the way Alexandrina would have. *Do you really think* you *deserve a prince?*

But Pia shoved that aside.

Right here, right now, he believed she was beautiful.

She didn't have to believe him to hold on to that for as long as she could.

For as long as he'd let her.

"Very well, then," she said, surrendering. Or, if she was honest, taking a leap into faith, despite everything. And having no idea where she might land. "I will do it, Ares. I will marry you."

Ares didn't realize until Pia finally agreed to marry him that a part of him had worried that she would not. That she would actually refuse him.

And it was one thing to make pronouncements about how he wished to live his life wifeless and childless and alone. It was another to be rendered such things because the woman he wanted would not have him.

But she had agreed at last. And he was ready—had been ready, in fact, since the day he'd met with his father and had decided on a different future.

And two days after Pia finally acquiesced, he found her on an achingly perfect morning by the sea, having her breakfast out on one of the palace's many terraces. For a moment he stood away from her, taking her in as she gazed out toward Kefalonia. This woman who had made him into a man he didn't recognize. A crown prince who wanted to claim his throne. A man who was no longer content to step aside for the father he had always hated.

Pia sat in the loose, flowing dress he had chosen for her, her dark hair back in a loose braid. The breeze from the ocean picked up strands and made them dance, this way and that, and he thought the sea itself paled beside her.

He could not believe she had ever imagined she was anything less than beautiful. Stunning, even.

He had met her mother. And he had found Alexandrina San Giacomo beautiful, yes, but brittle with it. Expectant. Her beauty was her currency, and she had been well aware of it. There was nothing wrong with that, to Ares's mind. He admired it, as he certainly knew when his own looks worked in his favor.

But Pia was beautiful in a different way altogether. Her beauty was unstudied. Artless. Her gray eyes were dreamy, her sweet mouth soft. Right now she was gloriously pregnant, ripe and lush, and it only added to her many charms.

Alexandrina had been a weapon. But Pia was a precious gem. As perfect as she was pretty.

And soon to be his princess. And one day, his queen.

He must have made a noise, because she glanced over then. And Ares had the pleasure of watching the way her eyes glowed with pleasure before she blinked it away to something far more guarded.

But the smile that curved her mouth was as bright and engaging as that first one back in New York.

It made something in him seem to turn over, then hum.

This one, a voice in him said, like some kind of gong. *This one*.

Mine, Ares thought.

He moved over to her, sliding a hand over her cheek and loving the way she leaned into his touch. The way she always did. She had no walls. She held nothing back.

She was heedless, hedonistic in bed, and he found that she made him insatiable.

There were no ways he didn't want her.

"I don't know what you have planned for today," he said.

Her gray eyes were soft and bright as she looked up at him. "I'm very busy, actually. I plan to lounge about, pretending to work, for several hours. After which I will very officiously go seat myself somewhere, open up the laptop, and type very studiously. I won't be working, of course. I'll be checking email and scrolling through things I don't care about on the internet, which is a very important part of my process. After several hours of that, I will write a single sentence, which will be so exhausting that I will instantly need to send for snacks. I plan to repeat this several times throughout the day, until I can break for an early dinner, and pretend none of it ever happened. And you?"

And that was the part Ares couldn't understand. He found her...entertaining.

He didn't understand it, but he liked it. True, he'd never seen anything like her before, anywhere in the royal family, or, for that matter, in any of the dreary noble houses of Europe. Everything was duty and history. Ancestral obligation and debts paid in to the future. Marriages were solemn contracts for the production of heirs, and everyone in those marriages worked hard to appear studiously joyless—if his own parents were any guide.

But the woman he would reign with was entertaining. She smiled, laughed. She even dared tease him. Ares chose to see it as a gift.

He went down before her, on the traditional single knee. Then he reached into his pocket, pulling out a small box with great flourish. He cracked it open, looking up to find Pia with her hands over her mouth and her gray eyes wide.

"I do not know if you recognize this ring," he said. "It has a legend attached to it. It was handed down through my family for generations, and each woman who wears it is said to be the queen the country deserves. Good, kind. It was my grandmother's. She left it for me when she died, that I might put it on the hand of my own queen one day. Will you take it?"

And he found that something in him was tense and tight until she let out a breath, nodded once, jerkily, and extended her hand that he might slide the ring into place.

Together, they stared down at the collection of three perfect sapphires, ringed with diamonds. Taken together the stones created the sense of something bigger than the sum of its parts. The ring itself was history. But on Pia, it looked like art.

"Thank you," she whispered, her voice catching. "It's so beautiful."

"I was hoping you would think so."

He helped her to her feet, aware that it was harder for her to rise these days. He swept his eye over the dress she wore, white and flowing, and making her look very nearly ethereal. He reached down to the table and picked up one of the flowers that sat there in a small vase, then tucked it into the top of her braid.

She was breathing loud enough that he could hear it. And her eyes were glassy when he was done with the flower. He wanted to lean down and kiss her, claim her—

But kissing Pia was no quick affair. It required time because Ares never stopped at one kiss. How could he?

"Come with me," he said.

And Pia held out her hand, because Pia always held out her hand. She trusted him enough to follow him into the unknown, and that was a responsibility Ares took seriously. More than seriously. He felt the weight of it move through him, and he vowed as he led her through the palace that he would honor it. Care for it.

And her.

Always her.

He hadn't planned for any of this. And he hadn't known, until that day in his father's study, how best to handle his impending fatherhood.

But now it was all so beautifully clear.

"What are we doing?" Pia asked, as he led her through the great salons and out to the wide terrace overlooking the steepest part of the rocky cliffs below. The ocean stretched itself in the sun, rambling out to the horizon. And there, beneath the makeshift canopy he'd had his staff prepare from sweet-smelling vines and bright flowers, a priest waited.

He felt her hand shake in his.

"Is this…?"

"This is our wedding, Pia," he said, looking down at her. Another tension gripping him because she could still balk. She could demand the cathedral on the Northern Island. She could refuse him. *She could still refuse him.* "Here, now."

"But…"

Ares took her hands in his. And he thought that he could lose himself forever in all that gleaming gray. He intended to. "Do you trust me?"

"I… I don't…"

"It's a simple question. You either trust me, or you do not."

"I trust you," she whispered.

"Then why wait?" he asked. "You know as well as I do what a royal wedding will be like. The pomp and circumstance, all in aid of a future throne. We can do this here. You and me, no one else. And our babies."

Her eyes glistened. Her smile seemed to tremble on her lips. Even her hands in his shook a little.

"Just you and me," she whispered.

There was a faint breeze from the sea spread out below them. The priest spoke his words, and when it was time for their vows, Pia had stopped shaking.

"I vow to honor you, keep you safe, and pledge my life to yours," Ares said, intoning the traditional vows of the kingdom.

"And I you," Pia replied.

He reached into his pocket and pulled out another box. Inside sat two rings. Two bands of gold. He slid the smaller one onto Pia's finger, so it sat flush against his grandmother's. And something dark and primitive roared through him at the sight.

He handed her the bigger ring and she took it, shifting her hand to slide it onto his finger.

And that was it, Ares thought. It was done.

"And now, Your Highness, you may kiss your bride," the priest declared.

And Pia was smiling again as he angled his face to hers, then took her mouth with his.

For a moment there was nothing but that kiss, sweet and perfect. Then another.

There was only the two of them, and the vows they'd made. Ares moved closer, pulling Pia further into his arms, because she was his. And he couldn't get enough of her.

And he doubted he ever would.

He kissed her again, deeper and wilder—

And that was when the helicopter rose up from below. It bristled with reporters, cameras in hand and pointing straight toward them.

Pia started to pull away, stiff with horror.

"Kiss me again," Ares commanded her.

"But the paparazzi—" she began.

"Kiss me, Pia," he told her, and he could hear the satisfaction in his own voice. He could feel it thrumming in his veins. He could very nearly picture the king's apoplectic rage when he saw these pictures—and understood what they meant. "I want them to see. I'm the one who called them here."

CHAPTER TWELVE

PIA DID AS Ares asked—as he commanded—because she could see no alternative.

And because she couldn't think. She kissed him, and the helicopter was right there, and everything was whipping around while she knew there were pictures being taken—

She was sure she could hear them laughing already.

Before she could object, or scream, or do any of the things that clambered inside of her and threatened to come out of her, violently—Ares pulled away. He shouted something to the priest over the noise of the helicopter's rotors.

He even waved.

Then he was leading her back inside the palace, leaving the helicopter and its paparazzi cargo behind. For a moment she let him lead her on, because she was too busy reeling to do anything else. She was blind and her heart *hurt* and it was a lie.

It was all a lie.

What had happened—what had just happened—hit her, hard.

I called them, he had said.

She dug her heels in, yanking her hand from his, and moving her hands around to the small of her back as she panted a little at the exertion and the low, dull pain that bloomed there. And she didn't know whether to look at him directly, or do her best to look away, maybe up and down the gallery where they'd stopped.

"What did you do?" she demanded. "What do you mean, you called them?"

"I called them," he said again, much too calmly for her peace of mind, and even looked a bit quizzical. As if she was the one who had stopped making sense in a dizzying rush.

And he was the man she loved. The man she had married in what she'd foolishly imagined was a quiet, sweet, personal ceremony.

She'd believed his *just the two of us*, and all the while he'd had a helicopter full of reporters waiting.

Which meant none of this had been romantic.

You knew better, she reminded herself bitterly. *And you did it anyway.*

Something in her turned over, spinning around in a nauseating loop. For a moment, she thought she might be sick. A kind of cramp ran through her, centering low in her belly, and she moved a hand to curl beneath the heaviest part of it. And she held it there, wishing she could hold herself together as easily.

"Tell me why," she managed to say. "Tell me why you would do this. We ran away from my father's funeral to avoid these people and you called them here… You must know that they took pictures that will be everywhere within the hour."

He raised a brow. "That was my clear intent."

Pia looked around, wildly, because she thought her legs might cease to hold her. There was a bench to the side, beneath a huge painting that she had studied in finishing school, the better to make sparkling cocktail conversation. She waddled over to the bench and sank down on to it. Gratefully.

Though she looked at Ares—her *husband*—and that awful feeling in her belly got worse.

"I do not understand why you are looking at me as if I killed a man," Ares said.

And what struck her most was how truly, effortlessly beautiful he was. He was dressed in one of his usual royal uniforms, complete with the sash that proclaimed him the crown prince of these islands. Even here, in a controlled environment with less intrusive lighting, he looked as if the sun beamed down upon him.

Pia should have known when Marbella had laid this particular dress out this morning. It was pure white. And while the hilarity of wearing all white while this astonishingly pregnant did not escape her, she couldn't quite bring herself to laugh.

Because she had believed him, and he had been putting on a show.

And all the things she'd told herself about the heartache she'd experience had been *one day*. Far off the future. Far away from here, now, *today*.

Yet here she was anyway, with a fantasy ring on her finger and a fantasy man, and a fantasy new marriage, too. The reality was a girl the size of a whale in a white dress that seemed pointed, a staged kiss, and all the sniggering she was sure she could already hear out there— or maybe her ears were ringing. She couldn't quite tell.

"I've spent my whole life in my father's shadow," Ares was telling her, standing over her with all that *light* he made on his own, and Pia should never have let herself do this. She should never have been so weak, risking not only her own humiliation—but her sons'. "I've never been good enough for the man. He ranted at me about our bloodline until I wished I could reach my hand inside my own body, and exsanguinate myself to escape it. The only thing that worked was keeping myself away from him. Excusing myself from the damned bloodline. But then you came along and changed everything."

"And you felt the best way to celebrate this change was with the paparazzi?"

Pia felt raw inside. Torn wide-open.

And worst of all, like such a fool.

Because she'd believed him. She'd believed that not only did he care for her, not only did he want her, but that deep down—whether he knew it or not—he might even love her.

She had believed what she wanted to believe, clearly.

And Ares had been setting up a photo opportunity to get at his father.

"I realized the last time I saw my father that I have abdicated my responsibilities entirely where he is concerned," Ares told her, still standing where she'd left him in the middle of the wide hall. "And the closer we get to the birth of our own two sons, the more I realize what I owe not only them, but this kingdom. I think our subjects deserve better."

"Power infects," she said, sounding hollow to her own ears. "You told me that."

"Better to claim it, then," Ares replied, something flashing in his green eyes. He crossed to her, then crouched down to put himself at eye level. "Better that than to let it sit about, festering. I want to be the kind of king these princes—" he put his hand out to touch her belly, and for the first time she wanted to slap it away "—can look up to. No temper tantrums like winter storms, brutal and unpredictable. No shards of crystal littering the floors while they stand there, hoping not to be hit. I want to be a better man, Pia."

There was a roaring thing in her, grief and shame, and she wasn't sure she could keep it inside her skin. She wasn't sure she could survive this. Or that she wanted to.

"You're not talking about being a better man, Ares," she threw back at him. "You're talking about being a king. You begged me to marry you, and I surrendered. You didn't tell me that it would be a business arrangement. You didn't convince me by promising me a convenient union we could both use to our own ends. You made love to me. You made it *romantic*."

And she would hate herself forever for the way her voice cracked on that.

But she pushed on anyway. "How could you make it romantic?"

Ares looked floored. Astounded, as if it had never occurred to him that she could possibly have a problem with what had happened here today.

"I do not understand the issue," he said stiffly.

"You could have asked me. You could have appealed to my practical side. You didn't have to *sleep* your way into it." And there were tears then, and those were worse. They felt too salty against her cheeks. They felt like a betrayal, or one more betrayal, and her heart felt tattered. Broken beyond repair. "You could have asked, Ares, and I would have come around."

"Pia—"

"But you pretended it was something else," she said, and the cramping was getting worse with every word she spoke. She rubbed at her belly, sucking in a breath as she tried to make herself comfortable. Or just make it through this conversation. "You pretended that you cared."

"I do care."

"You even told me I was beautiful." And her voice dropped on that, into something so painful it hurt her to hear herself. "Why did you have to lie to me? Has this whole thing been a game to you from the start?"

"This is not a game." He rocked back on his heels, and even now, the moment he stopped touching her she wanted only for him to start again. "How can you think it?"

"How could I think anything else?"

"I don't know what this is, Pia. Of course I care for you. You are the mother to my—"

"You told me I was beautiful," she said again, and her eyes were too blurry to see him now, which she took as a kind of blessing. There was a strange fire low in her belly, and that cramping that wouldn't stop. "And the worst thing is, I wanted to believe you. I did believe you. Why would you do this to me?"

"What did I do to you?" he roared at her, as if even now, he didn't understand.

"You made me think that you could love me," she

told him, though she thought it might kill her. There was a sob in her voice, and something heavy, like a stone, over her heart. And yet she kept going, though her face twisted. "Because only a man who loved me could find me beautiful."

Ares's face changed then, into something like alarm, and that was even worse. "Pia."

But she'd started down this road. She'd humiliated herself. Why not throw all her cards on the table? After all, what was there left to protect?

"I love you," she told him, sealing her doom. "And I never would have told you that. I would have kept it to myself because I know better. I still know better. But you told me I was beautiful, and I hoped, and you gave me your grandmother's ring. And I wanted so badly to believe it could all be real."

He moved closer to her, a harsh look she'd never seen before on his face. "Pia, you need to—"

She lifted up her hand to keep him back, because she couldn't trust herself. And she tried to struggle to her feet, but her legs refused to help her. And she reminded herself that no one actually died of heartache, no matter how terrible they felt. No matter how awful *she* felt right now.

"It's not the first time I've been made a fool of, and I doubt it will be the last," she told him. "You have what really matters to you. Legitimacy for your heirs. But I need you to promise me something, Ares. No matter what, you must never lie to me again. I need you to promise me that whatever games you need to play, it will never be this one. Never again."

"I will promise you anything you want, woman,"

Ares all but shouted at her. "But right now, you are bleeding."

It seemed to take Pia a lifetime or two to look down at the white dress she wore. The way it pooled around her feet.

And at the way what she'd taken for anxious cramps and heartache was instead bright red, and spreading out across her lap.

"Promise me," she said, though she didn't mean the same thing any longer. Or she didn't think she did.

But then it didn't matter what she meant, because the darkness came rushing at her, and sucked her in deep.

There was too much blood.

Ares caught Pia as she began to slump over, and he was already shouting for his staff. For someone to call back that damned helicopter. For help.

But there was blood. Everywhere.

He swung Pia up and into his arms, and he barely felt the weight she carried in that marvelous belly of hers. He strode toward the staff who yelled at him, or for him, he didn't care which.

Her face was so pale. And the blood kept coming.

It was the longest helicopter ride of his life. And when they landed on the Northern Island, on the top of the Royal Hospital, Ares was still holding her. And found he wanted to start knocking heads together, or start tearing people apart—*something*—when the medical personnel that met them on the roof took her from him to strap her on a gurney.

"She is my wife," he told them, aware he must sound mad with terror, with grief. Fierce with the fear that burned in him. "She will one day be your queen. She is carrying the heirs to this kingdom and you must save her. *You must.*"

And then, despite all his arrogance, all his consequence and power, he could do nothing but watch them rush her away.

Someone led him to a private room, eventually. They offered him a change of clothes, but he refused it. He sat in a chair with his head in his hands, and he waited.

While inside, his heart threatened to burst.

He could not lose Pia. He could not lose his sons.

He had spent his whole life doing everything he could to avoid having a family, and he was about to lose his before he got the chance to enjoy them.

Pia couldn't believe he had called her beautiful.

But Ares couldn't believe she loved him.

His first reaction was denial. Rage, that she would take this there, when it had worked fine as it was.

Because he knew what no one dared say to his face.

That there was nothing about him anyone could love, except his mother. And she had died a long time ago now.

But there was no one else on this earth, not even his father, who shared that sentiment. Ares was a monument to a throne, that was all. He was not a person. He existed in the first place only because his father needed an heir. Any child his mother had could have taken on that role. But no one *loved* him.

Except Pia.

And Ares could argue with himself all he liked. He could tell himself that she was mistaken. Or that she

didn't know enough about men and had fallen for the
first man who had ever touched her—

But he knew that wasn't true. There had been any
number of men at that party, but Pia had smiled at him.

Him.

Ares knew now that she had never done anything like
what she had that night in New York, but she'd done it
for him. She'd given him her innocence. She had suf-
fered his reaction to the news that she was pregnant.
She'd come with him to the islands, and allowed him
to lock her away for his own peace of mind, not hers.

She had done all these things, and he knew that there
could only be one reason. The one reason he never
would have come up with on his own, because the word
wasn't in his vocabulary.

She loved him.

Once he understood that, Ares couldn't understand
how he had ever managed to convince himself that it
was anything else. That it could be anything else.

And now she had blood all over her. Blood, again.
Blood always.

And if that blood was poisoned, the way he'd always
believed, he had done that, too.

And Ares found that while he had no trouble thinking of the ways he could pay for the sins of that bloodline, he couldn't bring himself to imagine that Pia might
also pay that price. Or either one of the babies she carried.

He could not lose her.

God help him, he could not lose her, not now. Not
when he had only begun to grasp how very much she
meant to him.

She was the only woman he had ever been this intimate with. There was the astonishingly good sex, yes, but they'd spent all this *time* together. Time enough to get to know her. Time enough to understand how much more it was he wanted to know her.

Time to understand that he wanted, badly, to meet his own sons.

Ares needed more time.

He thought he could spend a lifetime trying to imagine what Pia might say next. He thought he could spend another one learning the different shades of meaning in her smiles.

She was the only woman he had given his grandmother's ring. The only woman he had asked to marry him, not once, but time and time again.

She was the only woman, period.

She needed to live, so he could tell her so. So he could tell her a thousand things. So he could apologize for treating her like a pawn—

She just needed to *live*.

"Your Highness," came a voice from a doctor at the door, and Ares's head shot up, but he couldn't read anything on the man's face. "Your wife is stable, but the babies are in some distress. We will be performing a cesarean section immediately."

"Early," Ares managed to say, his head spinning. "It's too early."

"Twins are always early," the doctor replied. "But we must make haste."

And Ares followed, unable to do anything else.

Because he could not lose Pia. And he could not lose these babies he had yet to meet. And he had not realized until now, until he found himself in these antiseptic halls, how very thoroughly lost he had been since the first moment he'd set eyes on this woman.

His wife.

His future queen, and mother to the future king of Atilia.

Ares, by God, would make sure she lived long enough to assume each and every one of those roles.

And tell him she loved him once more.

CHAPTER THIRTEEN

PIA WOKE UP in a panic. A desperate, confused rush—

"Pia. *Cara mia.*"

Her head snapped around, and she found him there. *Ares.*

With those grave green eyes, and a stern set to his beautiful mouth. Ares, her prince, though he appeared to be wearing hospital scrubs. Of all things.

She felt herself calm, just a little. Because Ares was there, and that meant—

"My babies—" she blurted out, her heart exploding inside her. She tried to sit up, but her abdomen protested sharply, and she had the terrible notion that she'd had surgery. And that meant… "What happened to my babies—"

"We have all been waiting for you," Ares said, very solemnly, and the calm sound of his voice made her stop. Made her breathe. "Allow me to make the introductions."

And then he reached into the double bassinet she hadn't seen beside the bed, and carefully lifted up a tiny little bundle. It sported a wrinkled pink face and a shock of dark hair peeking out from beneath a little white beanie.

"I present to you our first born," Ares said, something rich and awed in his voice. "He is perfect in every way. I inspected him myself."

Pia accepted her baby, a rush of something so intense and primitive slamming into her as she took him that she was happy—fiercely so—she was already in a bed. Because she feared it would have knocked her over. She gazed down at the tiny bundle in her arms, making sounds she hadn't heard herself make before. She saw him scrunch up his nose, and his perfect little mouth, and she understood that she would never be the same again.

"And his brother," Ares said, and placed the other baby in her other arm. As if he knew that she needed to touch them both. "He is equally perfect in every way. I can verify this personally."

And that same wave took her over again. Harder, deeper.

She bent her head to one, then the other. She checked to make sure each one was breathing. And as she did, each tiny boy began to make tiny little noises, as if they understood exactly who she was and were offering their own form of greeting.

She could already tell they were that smart. That beautiful. That absolutely perfect.

"You were there?" she asked.

"They came out of you, directly into my hands," Ares said, and it sounded like another vow. Like an impossible intimacy.

And when she met his gaze, her chest ached.

"I want to feed them," she whispered.

Or, having missed their birth, maybe she needed to.

And Ares was there beside her, so she didn't have to worry over all the various things she'd read about how best to get each one of them where they needed to go. He helped her. He set a pillow over her abdomen, which stuck out significantly less than it had when she'd last seen it.

He opened up her gown, and he helped her guide one greedy mouth to her swollen, aching breast. Then the next, placing each little body beneath one of her arms, snug against her sides, so she could hold them in place like American footballs.

And she had read a thousand articles about how difficult breastfeeding was, and had read endless forums about how to manage it with hungry twins. She'd expected a battle. But there was no battle to mount, because it was happening. She felt one twin latch on, then the other. And they both began to pull at her.

Pia looked up at Ares while each of the perfect creatures they'd made together fed from her breasts, and she understood what family was on a primitive level she'd never imagined existed before.

She had known love. She had loved. She was still in love with the maddening man who stood beside her.

This was something else, this communion between the four of them. This needed a new word. This was like a new sun, bright and hot inside of her, taking her over, burning her up, terrifying and magical—and it was theirs.

They had done this. They had made this happen.

Nothing would ever be the same. But at the same time, everything was finally…beautiful.

And when the babies were fed and she and Ares had

held each of them against their bare skin a while, a nurse came in to check them again, then whisked them off for more tests. Pia tried to move in her bed, winced at the pain from her abdomen, and realized that she still didn't know what had happened to her.

"I can tell you this story using all kinds of medical terminology," Ares said. "But what really matters is that I nearly lost you. And Pia. No matter how I let you down today, trust me when I tell you that losing you is unacceptable to me. It is unthinkable."

She stared back at him, and he told her quickly and matter-of-factly about the rush to get her to the hospital. Her hemorrhage, the emergency cesarean section. How close she'd come to dying, and how terrified he had been.

"You told me you loved me," he said, as he stood there next to her bed, stiff and tense, as if that was an insult.

And Pia didn't want to remember this part. Not when she was still filled with that perfect sense of overwhelming, impossible, helpless love. She didn't want to remember their wedding ceremony. That helicopter. All the cameras.

"It doesn't matter," she said now. "We're parents, Ares, to two perfect little boys in desperate need of names. Let's just concentrate on—"

"You told me you loved me, Pia," Ares thundered at her. "And no one has told me that before, not unless they'd given birth to me themselves. That isn't the kind of thing you can just *say* to a man."

She wanted to cry again. "I'm sorry if I insulted you."

"I have spent the last five hours begging gods I've

never believed in to save you," he told her then, tall and still golden. And he had held their babies in his hands when she couldn't. He had been there. "Our wedding photos are all over every paper in the land, just as I wished, and it is like ash to me. Because there is no point in any of this, Pia, unless you are here. With me."

"Ares…"

"I have no idea how to love anyone," he told her, his green eyes blazing. "But for you, I will learn. I have no idea what a father does except crush his own son, but for the ones we made, I will learn how to do it right."

He moved closer, taking her hands in his, and then going down on one knee beside her hospital bed.

"You don't have to do this, Ares," she said.

"When I thought I would lose you, every moment we spent together went through my head in a rush," he said urgently. "And I could see it so clearly then, how much you loved me. How much you have always loved me. And how much I have failed you, time and again."

"No," she said fiercely. She winced as she sat up, but she reached out and took his beautiful, beloved face in her hands. "You are not a failure, Ares. I love you. That's not conditional on how you behave. That doesn't come with a list of duties or expectations. I just love you. It's as simple and as complicated as that, and I don't know how it works, either."

"I used you like a pawn. I will never forgive myself."

"I already have," she said, and as the words came out of her, she realized they were true. "I've spent my whole life hating how I looked because I wasn't my mother. Hating my body because it never looked like hers. But look what it did today."

"You were magnificent," Ares told her, his voice thick. "You are always magnificent, Pia."

"Let them laugh if they like," Pia said, her eyes on Ares. "They don't matter. They never did. The only thing I have to be embarrassed about is that I ever let them get to me in the first place. Even in my own head."

His mouth formed her name, but he turned his head so he could kiss her palm.

"I spent my whole life watching my parents tear themselves apart and call it love," Pia told him, a new conviction growing inside her. As if it had always been there. As if her babies' arrival had jogged it loose. "I used to think that was romantic. Now I suspect it was deeply unhealthy. What I want with you is the chance to explore the difference."

"I love you," Ares told her. "And I will spend the rest of this life proving to you that it's not only because I thought I would lose you today. But because in thinking you were lost to me forever, I understood that forever was meaningless to me without you."

"We made them," she whispered. "And Ares. They're perfect."

"They're beautiful," he whispered back. "And so are you."

And for a moment they grinned at each other, wide and bright and brimming with hope and possibility. There were two new, shiny little lives, and both of them would do their best to protect each one of them. To honor them and raise them.

Together.

"Pia," Ares said, a quiet command. "Be my wife."

"It will be my greatest honor," she said, tears streaming down her face, but this time, they were not tears of pain. This was joy, this unwieldy, unsteady thing that held her in so tight a grip. *Pure joy.* "And you must be my husband."

"It will be my privilege," he said solemnly. "You will be my queen one day. But know this, Pia. You are already, and always will be, queen of my heart."

And when he leaned over and pressed his mouth to hers, Pia tasted salt and sweetness. The great tangle that led to forever, and all the knots they'd tied in each other already that would keep them steady and connected as they headed there.

He kissed her, and it was like a fairy tale.

He kissed her, and she kissed him, and they woke each other up from that deep, dark enchantment that was the lives they'd led without each other.

Without love.

There and then, in a hospital room with the paparazzi calling their names outside, they started their new life. Together.

Full of love, light, and laughter to hold it all together, like glue.

Twenty years later, six weeks after his father's death and his formal acceptance of his new role, King Ares of Atilia was crowned in the Great Cathedral.

He took the long walk up the cathedral's august aisle that he had believed, once, he would never take.

The crowd cheered for him outside. The Atilian nobles and European aristocrats filled the pews. The famous Atilian choir sang ancient songs of power and glory.

But Ares's gaze was on his family.

His fine, strong twins, Crown Prince Pollux and Prince Castor, who stared back at him with pride and love—something Ares had done his best to earn every day for two decades. Beside them, the rest of his children stood tall. His middle children, seventeen-year-old Leto and thirteen-year-old Nyx. And his second set of twins, his mischievous ten-year-old daughters, Helen and Clytemnestra, who looked like the young women they would become someday.

Someday, Ares thought as they beamed at him, but not today. No need to rush into it.

He had never built any significant bridges with his father, who had divorced and married twice more, but had never produced another child. The old king had died in a fury, and had been found with crystal shards all around him like a halo. Ares figured that was as close as Damascus was likely to get to the good place.

The older he got, the more Ares wished he could have worked things out with the man, but he understood the ache of it had more to do with his relationship with his own children. And the man he hoped he was in their eyes, the father he was first and always, before he was a king.

And when he talked to them about bloodlines, what he talked about was love.

Ares kept walking, taking in Pia's brothers as they stood in the row behind his children. Because they were important to Pia, Ares had made them important to him, too. And as the years passed, he found Matteo Combe and Dominik James were more to him than a duty. They became more like…brothers.

And as all their families grew, with sets of twins to

go around, it was hard to remember that Matteo was the one who had punched Ares at that funeral. Or that there was ever a time that Pia didn't refer to her sisters-in-law, the impressive Dr. Sarina Fellows Combe and high-level Combe Industries executive Lauren Clarke James, as not only her sisters, but her friends.

With every step he took, Ares counted the ways he was a lucky man.

He had been born a prince, but it had taken Pia to make him a man. And it was only with Pia by his side that he could take his throne and become a king.

Ares reached the front of the cathedral and climbed the short stairs, then bent his head to accept the priests' invocations.

He thought about his kingdom. About the Southern Palace that rarely stood empty these days, and more often rang with life and laughter, as it was meant to do. He thought about his people, who had accepted it when he'd told them that he'd kept his relationship with Pia secret because the two of them had needed a time that was only theirs.

And most of all, he thought of the woman who was there at his side when the priests placed the crown on his head, then handed him the ceremonial scepter.

He watched as they fit her with a crown of her own, but her gray eyes shined brighter than any crown. Especially when she looked at him and smiled.

Ares held out his hand to her, breaking ancient custom.

And Pia took it, because she always did.

Because she trusted him. She loved him.

And the way he loved her in return would have scared him, if she didn't meet it so fiercely, so fully.

The only war he'd ever fought had been against himself, and Pia had taught him how to put down his arms.

He lifted her hand to his mouth.

"You have accepted the crown of the kingdom, and I have made you my queen," he said.

"You have."

"But there is a greater role for you to play," he told her, knowing his voice carried not only to the furthest corners of the Great Cathedral, but was being heard on television sets and radios around the world. "You are the most beautiful thing I have ever beheld. I count myself lucky every day I get to spend with you. You have made me a better man, and in so doing, will help me be the fair and just ruler my people deserve."

Her eyes gleamed with unshed tears. She whispered his name.

"I promised you a long time ago that this day would come," he said, and let himself grin, there before his children, his extended family, his subjects, and the planet. "Pia, love of my life, will you wield your crown not only as the queen of Atilia, but as the queen of My Heart?"

She stepped back, smiling, and then executed a perfect, deep curtsy.

"Your Majesty," she said, distinct and sweet, while the gleam in her gaze promised him a long, hot night ahead, "it will be my pleasure."

Ares kissed her when she rose, as if this coronation were the wedding day he and Pia had kept to themselves, and were now, finally sharing with the world. And she kissed him back as if they were alone.

The priests finished their blessings. And the roar of the crowd outside made the stained glass shake.

And then, when it was done and the bells began to toll, King Ares of Atilia took his beautiful queen by the hand, and led her into their sweet, bright, happy future. Just like those fairy tales Pia had mentioned all those years ago, when they were new.

Ares was the king. He would make it so. He would make it beautiful, like her.

For her.

And day by day, year by year, that was exactly what he did.

* * * * *

LET'S TALK
Romance

For exclusive extracts, competitions
and special offers, find us online:

- **f** facebook.com/millsandboon
- **◎** @millsandboonuk
- **🐦** @millsandboon

Or get in touch on 0844 844 1351*

For all the latest titles coming soon,
visit millsandboon.co.uk/nextmonth